THEIR PATH TO HAPPINESS

JENNIFER DEUTSCH

Joshua Tree Publishing

• Chicago •

THEIR PATH TO HAPPINESS
JENNIFER DEUTSCH

Published by
Joshua Tree Publishing
• Chicago •
JoshuaTreePublishing.com

13-Digit Print ISBN: 978-1-956823-39-4

Cover Image Credit: Pavlo Klymenko, Adobe Stock

Disclaimer:
This is a work of fiction. Names, characters, places, and incidents are the product of the author's imagination or have been used fictitiously. Any resemblance to actual persons, living or dead, events, locales or organizations is entirely coincidental.

Printed in the United States of America

DEDICATION

To those who have told me,
"I am worth it" and to those who have said, "I'm not."
Most importantly, to my family,
who have supported me through it all,
making it hard for me to give up on myself.
We have had our ups and downs,
but I wouldn't trade my company on this journey
I call life with any other crew!
I love you to the moon and back,

KMMLEBWBDJT

DEDICATION

CHAPTER 1

The rain poured on the roof before the first light of day, and a low rumble of thunder could be heard in the distance. Kaleigh tossed and turned in her sleep, her mind racing with thoughts of a car crash on a stormy night. And, just as every time she had this dream, she awoke as the car made impact with a tree. Kaleigh sat up abruptly, her breath heavy, and then realized it had all been just a dream.

As usual, when this scary dream occurred, it took her some time to calm her breathing. After a few minutes, she got out of bed and walked to the kitchen for a drink of water. On this night, she passed by the piles of schoolwork, a stack of bills, a greenhouse lease that her dad had asked her to review, and her computer as she made her way to the sink. She put a small glass under the faucet, lifted the handle as she took a deep breath, and filled the cup with water. As she sipped the cool water, she rubbed the back of her neck, feeling the knot that, lately, had never seemed to go away. Then, after a few minutes, she slowly walked back to bed, setting her glass on the bedside table.

The next thing Kaleigh knew, her alarm was going off, and she heard the soft rain falling gently on the window. She stretched and reluctantly sat up to begin her day. As she rummaged through her messy closet, getting dressed, her phone rang.

It was her brother, Wesley. She could barely say "Good morning," when he interrupted her. "Hey, I need you to take Dad to his one-o'clock appointment today."

"What, today?" Kaleigh replied, trying not to sound annoyed. Lately, her brother had been asking her for favors at the last minute more and more often. As a school teacher, this always put her in a difficult position.

"Yes, his doctor wants to see him for a check-up to go over his latest tests, and I have a very important meeting that has come up," Wesley spoke in a quick and matter-of-fact tone.

"I can't. I have my observation at twelve-thirty today. It's for my fifth-period class that doesn't let out until one-fifteen."

"Fine, I'll figure something out!" Wesley quickly said and hung up.

Kaleigh let out a sigh, put her phone in her pocket, chose a blue blouse and matching flats, and headed toward the bathroom.

At that moment, her friend Danielle texted her, and she quickly checked her phone.

"Latte?"

"Absolutely," she replied. She finished getting ready and then quickly headed toward the kitchen. As she filled her lunch bag with her usual yogurt, granola bar, and apple, her heart sank as she stared at the pile of ungraded papers. She chose one stack to throw in her bag with her laptop, hoping she could manage to get some of them graded during her free period. Then she reached into the fridge one more time for a bottle of water and headed out the door.

****

In the staff room, Kaleigh met her best friend, Danielle, who handed her a warm cup of delicious caramel flavor.

"You're a lifesaver," Kaleigh said with a hesitant smile, taking a deep breath over the lid of the coffee cup, trying to relax a little.

"Are you OK?" her best friend asked.

"It's Wes. He's frustrated with me because I can't take Dad to an appointment today . . . He called an hour ago to ask me . . . I'm just so stressed. There's just so much to do, and I'm pulled in so many directions. And this observation today . . ." Kaleigh trailed off as she rubbed her now-pounding head.

"Don't worry about that. You're a natural. You'll do great. Did you finish the PowerPoint?"

"Yes, at least that is ready. I just wish Wes had made Dad's appointment for later this afternoon. He knows I can't do one o'clock," Kaleigh replied as she rubbed her head once more.

"Here, take these," Danielle said as she handed her some headache medicine just as the bell rang. "Here they come. Let me know if you need anything today."

"Thanks, Dani. You're the best."

Looking at the clock, she realized she had fifteen minutes before her first period class began. She walked slowly to her classroom and sat down at her desk. Kaleigh did not typically sit much throughout the day, but now, in this moment of quiet, she sat back in her chair, taking turns sipping her coffee and resting her eyes. She tried not to replay this morning's conversation with Wesley in her head, but it was tough.

After each period ended, she continued to replay the conversation, knowing there was no way she could have made the appointment with Dad today, but was second- guessing herself anyway. Should she have changed her observation and taken the afternoon off? None of these back-and-forth thoughts helped her headache at all, and by lunchtime, she found herself taking more medicine. She made sure to eat her lunch, hoping that would help her head and her stress level. Having a growling stomach during the observation by her principal would not have been a great idea. Somehow, Kaleigh needed to find a way to slow her mind down and relax.

****

At 12:30 p.m., Kaleigh's observation began. She introduced her lesson on creating a dominant character with clear personality traits that would help lead her writers to build a strong story. The slides she had created were interactive, and the students took turns choosing various personality traits their characters could have. Based on those traits, the program would help lead her students in the direction their possible story could go. The students were all engaged as it was something new that they had not done before. They were able to voice their opinions and ideas as Kaleigh took them through the slides, showing them how varied their stories could be, depending on the personality traits they chose for their leading character. The newness of the activity, and the amazing interactive technology that Kaleigh had put together, really helped the students see a story coming to life. All of this made for very interesting discussions.

After a few minutes, Kaleigh shared the slideshow virtually with her students and let them explore it. Their job was to play around with the slideshow to get an idea of where they wanted to go with their story character. Kaleigh circulated the room and helped answer some questions. She was excited to see even her most difficult student playing around with the slideshow and getting to work. Kaleigh stopped at his desk to answer a very thoughtful question. She could tell he was motivated by this assignment. Then she spent the last few minutes of class asking some thought-provoking questions to a group of three students, getting them to think ahead to their story idea and what kind of character would fit best. All the while, the principal smiled as she typed on her computer, listening intently to what both Kaleigh and her students were saying.

With one minute left in class, the phone rang. It was Debbi from the main office. Kaleigh answered the phone. She listened intently to the words Debbi was saying but couldn't say a word. Just as the bell rang, Kaleigh dropped the phone on the floor. From across the hall, Danielle saw the phone drop to the floor, and both she and the principal came running over, helping her sit down at her desk chair as the students closed their computers, gathered their belongings, and left the room.

One of the students, Savannah, stopped to ask if her teacher was alright. Danielle thanked her for her concern and assured her that Ms. Evans would be fine. Then she asked her to close the door on her way out so that no students would enter the room. Seeing a tear fall from her friend's face, Danielle handed her a tissue and held her hand.

Chapter 2

As Kaleigh peeked through the office door, she said, "Hey, Dad. There you are. I'm here to help you with the plantings today."

"Oh my, Leigh. You are so sweet to come and help your old man every Saturday when I'm sure you have more important things to do." Her dad always had the best smile and was so proud of all she had accomplished, even though her career led her away from the family's Garden Center. He wanted her to be happy and to follow her own path, and he never pressured either of his kids to follow in his footsteps.

"There is no place I'd rather be," Kaleigh said as she reached from behind and gave him a hug. "You know, since we lost Mom, it has been nice spending these few hours a week with you."

"Oh, sweetheart, I feel the same way. I know it's been tough."

"That's why I'm here. I know Wes has a lot going on running the front end and handling the staff, the restocking, and the ordering."

"Yes, he does. He really has been an asset to me and to the store, and so have you." After pausing for a moment, he added, "Are you ready?"

"Yep," she said, and they gathered buckets and shovels and headed to the truck. They would spend the next few hours potting beautiful flowers from the greenhouse and bringing them into the store for sale.

Later that day, just when Kaleigh was cleaning up the back room before heading home, Wesley stopped her.

"Hey, Steve called out again. Do you think you could help me close?"

Kaleigh was looking forward to curling up on her couch after a shower and grading papers by the fireplace, but after a pause, she sighed and said, "Sure."

"Thanks, you're a lifesaver. I'll meet you up front. We've been pretty busy today," he said, dashing away. Kaleigh had gotten used to saving the day lately. She often stayed late on Saturdays to help her brother run the store. Dad was beginning to slow down, finding it harder and harder to get the same amount of work done as he used to. He was hesitant to hire more people even though the Garden Center was doing well and making a good profit each month. She had talked to Dad about hiring more help, but he just wasn't ready to take that step. He wanted to make sure that they stayed in the black, as he never knew how business might fluctuate in the future. Although Dad was slowing down and unable to work the ten to twelve hours per day that he used to, he felt he was still strong enough to handle most tasks around the center with shorter shifts.

Each month that went by, Wesley added a little more to his plate, whenever he noticed that dad hadn't gotten around to doing something. Every week Kaleigh continued to come and help her dad with the flowers, shrubs, and greenery, as well as little tasks around his house such as cleaning, which he was no longer able to keep up with.

Then, one Saturday morning, everything began to change.

Dad was climbing a ladder just as Kaleigh walked into the storeroom. The lace of his shoe got stuck. As he tried to wiggle his shoe free, he slipped, fell to the ground, and let out a painful cry. Kaleigh immediately worried that he had hit his head hard on the concrete, but Dad was screaming out in pain and holding his leg. Kaleigh had only seen her dad cry once in her life, on the day three years before when Mom had suddenly passed away. After an ambulance ride to the hospital, it was discovered that Dad had broken his left leg badly. His hospital stay lasted for almost two weeks. After that, he spent two more weeks in a rehabilitation center and then had a visiting nurse for another four weeks while he recovered at home.

The accident happened at the start of summer. It was after Kaleigh's first year of teaching, so she ended up working overtime, trying to keep up with everything her father would have taken care of. She jumped in without even being asked and helped her brother run the store. There was no vacation, no day off, just jumping in to help wherever needed. The Garden Center was her legacy, too, and she felt that it was her duty to step in and help while her father was out of commission. Thankfully, it was summer, and school was not in session.

That was the summer she worked with Jackson, a local farmer who had been asking to sell some of his produce at their Garden Center. Dad was never sure he wanted to change things. They had never sold fresh fruits and vegetables, just fresh plants and herbs and everything you would ever need to landscape your house or start a small garden. Dad hadn't wanted to mess with a good thing. He liked that they had kept the business just as his dad had built it.

While Dad was in rehab, learning how to get around on crutches, Kaleigh had talked Wesley into giving fresh produce sales a try. She had worked one weekend with their carpenter to build two large tables for the front of the store. They had decided on a four-week trial to see if business improved and if the sales of the produce were worth the effort. It turned out the extended business the Garden Center received for the first week of the produce sales had been a success, and the sales each week moving forward were better than the last. When Dad returned to work, he might have been a little upset at his children going behind his back to try something he had originally said no to, but he tried not to show it. He did not want to seem ungrateful for all his they had done while he was unable to work. He came around when he saw the added business that this new endeavor brought to the store. Business was up, and some of the customers came up to him and complimented the change.

Jackson was a long-time family friend. He had known Kaleigh and Wesley through their school-age years and the three of them had some great memories together. Jackson didn't know if his excitement was about beginning a business relationship with the Garden Center, or getting the chance to see Kaleigh more, or maybe both.

Jackson had come back that Saturday night after the carpenter went home and had offered to help Kaleigh sand and stain the new produce tables. They talked for hours and laughed as they reminisced of the past and talked about what their peers from high school had been up to since graduation. He had ordered dinner from the local diner, and the two had a good time. Jackson had gone to school with Wesley. Kaleigh, who was two years older than the boys, hung out a lot with them in high school. They each spent time at each other's houses all those years ago and knew each other well.

Jackson's father owned the farm that he now was quickly taking over, the same place Wesley had been finding himself in lately. They talked, laughed, and smiled, and, for a brief moment, Kaleigh was able to let go of all her worries. Jackson's company was just what she needed at that moment. He was like a brother to her, and they had been friends for years. However, with Kaleigh's new job, she had not seen him as much lately. Jackson had missed seeing her and was happy to have this chance to catch up. Once they finished staining the tables, Kaleigh was so tired that Jackson offered to drive her home.

After Dad's accident, even with all of these changes, Kaleigh and Wesley never really talked about who would take over the business. It kind of just happened. A few years back it was Kaleigh who had decided to go to college and become a teacher, and Wesley never seemed to have the desire to further his education. He had been working full-time at the Garden Center since he graduated from high school and eventually became the front-end manager when Lydia retired. At this point, it was just assumed that Wesley would take over the business. He continued to excel at most of the tasks and responsibilities that it took to run the store. He never complained. When there was something he had trouble with, he found someone to delegate the task to, and the store was doing very well.

CHAPTER 3

The first night that Dad was in the hospital after the fall, Danielle brought coffee and dinner, and the girls talked for over two hours. They had bonded that year, both finishing their first year of teaching English at Forest Grove Middle School. They shared some laughs, looking back at some of their most tricky students. Middle school students can be hard to reach, and it can be tough to build a bond with them, so they trust you. In order to be good teachers, the women knew how important it was to connect with their students and build that trust. Both Danielle and Kaleigh had proved to be good at building relationships with their students, and their hard work during their first year of teaching had paid off. They were both asked to return the next year, and the principal had asked them to work on making their English department and the courses that they offered even stronger. That was not to say that they didn't have some difficult days, though. But through it all they felt proud of their accomplishments and had become the best of friends.

On that same night, Wesley had come by the hospital for only fifteen minutes. He stayed just long enough to get an update on the surgery that Dad needed the next day, where the doctors would put two pins in his leg. Wesley was stern and noticeably upset. This was the first time that Kaleigh noticed a big change in her brother. His usual fun-loving personality and team spirit were beginning to fade, slowly being replaced by a stiff and serious man.

Kaleigh had been doing all she could to help at the store even on her busiest weeks of the school year. She stayed late on Saturdays whenever Wesley asked. She was the one who went to school to create a career for herself. It was Wesley who always stayed close to the store, and in all these years, had never complained. Kaleigh had always assumed that was what he wanted—to run the store on his own someday. Was he upset about dad's fall? Was he upset about dad being out of commission for a while? Or was he overwhelmed with all the responsibilities he now had to take on? Kaleigh wanted to ask her brother, but in his rushed and upset mood she felt that now was not the time.

Kaleigh's plan for a summer of rest ended the day of the fall. That summer, she often worked more than eight hours a day to help Wesley keep everything at the Garden Center running like clockwork. She did whatever she could to pick up any slack in whatever department and to take tasks off Wesley's plate whenever she could. Behind the scenes she was also taking care of dad's house, cleaning, shopping and making sure he had what he needed to be comfortable in his recovery. Kaleigh wasn't sure how much Wesley appreciated her help, but she showed up every day with a smile until it was time for Teacher Orientation. Kaleigh had to be at school four days per week now, as she prepared for a new school year. By then, thank goodness, Dad was back to work, albeit in a leg brace and on crutches, and only able to work around four to six hours per day.

It was then that Dad finally agreed to hire Teddy, a construction foreman who was looking for a change in career, and he quickly became Dad's right-hand man. Teddy was the perfect addition to the team and could handle the heavy lifting that Dad was unable to do on his own. The store looked great, the produce sales continued to be an amazing addition and the customers kept coming back for more. In looking back, Kaleigh felt like she had made a real difference that summer.

Ever since Dad returned from his accident, she had promised him that she would continue to work with him every Saturday morning, as she had done since Mom passed away. It was important to her that she was still supporting her father and the family business, even if it were only a few hours per week.

The accident that summer was the beginning of a series of gradual changes in Dad's health over the months and years to come. His mobility was never the same after the fall, and even after not needing the large leg brace, he often had to wear a small brace on his leg for extra support. His ability to kneel on the ground, take plants out of the soil, and plant them into pots was diminishing, and the pace at which he walked and worked was slowing more and more.

Teddy worked full-time at the Garden Center and helped Dad find a dependable part-time employee that would help lessen the workload. Between the three of them and the part-time high school students, they were able to keep up with planting, hauling and setting the plants, making them ready for purchase. This plan worked for a while, but then Dad's memory began fading, and he was less and less productive on the days on which he could make it to work.

First, there were little things he was forgetting, like where he left his calculator, which day each week he needed to be at the store early for a delivery, or where the keys to his truck were. Kaleigh got a call on many occasions to help solve these small problems, and for a while, she put some things in place that helped Dad with these day-to-day small forgetful moments. She set timers, left reminder notes, and had an extra set of keys made for his truck. She even ordered and installed a message center where reminder notes, keys, and mail could be kept. She set alarms on his phone for each day of the week, so he would know when to get up and when he needed to be at the store. This support helped Dad for a short time, but once he began to forget where he was, that was a real wake-up call. He called Kaleigh multiple times when he was lost, and she would get in her car to go find him. The day finally came when Kaleigh made the call to Wesley that she had been dreading.

"Hey, Wesley, do you have a minute?" she began.

"Yeah, I guess so. We're expecting a delivery in about five minutes, and I don't know where Dad is," Wesley replied.

"Well, that's what I need to talk to you about. You remember last week when Dad got lost while trying to go to the grocery store for the fourth time?" Kaleigh was trying to keep the tone light and not go into her worried voice. She had mentioned his forgetful moments here and there during their conversations at the store, but didn't feel that Wesley was bothered by these changes in Dad as much as she was.

"Yeah. Why?" Wesley's tone was rushed, and Kaleigh could hear that he was moving around the store.

"Well, since then, Dad has called me twice, trying to drive somewhere in the truck and lost track of where he was going—"

"So, we'll take the keys. Teddy can pick him up." Wesley spoke so fast he had interrupted her.

"No, it's more than that. He has fallen twice in three days at the house, and I think he is forgetting to eat dinner. I mean, I've left entrees for him to heat up each night, with reminder notes and directions, and when I went over after work last night, none of the dinners were touched. When I went over today, I found him in a weird position on the floor, like he had been there a while after falling."

"So, what are you saying?" Wesley said in a somewhat stern tone.

She carefully and quietly said the words, "It's time."

"Time for what?"

"I am meeting with a placement specialist at Havenwood. Dad can't be at home alone anymore. He needs to be somewhere with around-the-clock care." She paused before she said what she knew would be tough on Wesley, "And he won't be able to come to work anymore."

The conversation suddenly stopped, and everything got quiet. No one said anything for what seemed like an entire minute.

Finally, Wesley said in a slow voice, shocked that this moment had come so soon, "OK." Then, after another moment of silence, he abruptly said, "I gotta go," and hung up.

That next week, Kaleigh took two days off from work and moved her dad into Havenwood. Wesley kept his distance and let Kaleigh take the lead on everything with Dad. Kaleigh wasn't sure if it was because the store was so busy or because he did not want to see Dad in this state. She still hadn't had the conversation with Wesley about how he was feeling about things. Kaleigh made a mental note to find time to do that.

****

While Wesley took over the business, hiring more staff to help with the workload, Kaleigh was arranging everything for Dad, including the sale of the house and the sorting of all his belongings. She did this all while working full-time at school. She was so busy that during that time, she was unable to work at the Garden Center, and for a long time, she didn't see her brother. They would text or call each other when they needed help going with Dad to an appointment or when news had come in from one of his doctors, but that was all the conversation they had been having these last couple of years.

Except for one rainy night at the store, at closing time. Kaleigh came in just as the last customer was walking out and Wesley was pulling the last register drawer.

"Hey Wes," she said as she gave him a wave. "Are you up for a drink at Rita's?" she paused, not knowing what his response would be. As he walked back toward the office, she followed behind him, though not too closely.

After a few moments Wesley replied, "OK."

The two drove in separate cars down the the tavern, then sat at a table in a quiet section of the restaurant. After ordering drinks and an appetizer, Kaleigh noticed the silence and quickly realized that she would need to break the ice.

"Hey Wesley, I just wanted to say that I miss you. With everything that has gone on lately, there just hasn't been time for you and me to catch up, you know, talk, like we used to."

"Yeah, I know. The store is just so busy." Was all Wesley could say at that moment.

"Well, how are you?" Kaleigh continued, hoping he felt like he could share something with her in this moment.

"I'm okay," he replied. "I guess I am just living my new normal, in charge of the store, every day." Then there was silence as the waitress brought their drinks and left.

This was it. This was the time to ask the question she had been wanting to ask for so long. "Is that what you want, to be in charge of the store?"

Again, more silence. Wesley took a long sip of his beer, then used his napkin to wipe the condensation off of the table, not looking up at all. Kaleigh decided the best thing to do was to let him think in this moment, so she stayed quiet.

Finally, Wesley answered, "It's what I need to do." Then he paused again, looking into his beer, and continued, "It's all I have."

After waiting another minute in silence, Kaleigh said, "I just want you to be happy, to do something you love." She paused a moment, then added, "I want you to have fun outside of work, to find someone who makes you laugh, and to be happy with your life. And if you're not, I hope that you know you can tell me. It's okay."

Just then the appetizers came, and they began to eat. Wesley had not eaten much today and suddenly realized that he was famished. He never did answer Kaleigh's question, but it had given him a lot to think about.

Nothing else was said about the store that night. Kaleigh felt that she shouldn't press the issue anymore. They talked about how great Teddy was, how the sales continued to grow with the new commercial that was running on television, which was Teddy's idea. Then they touched briefly on Dad. Wesley didn't say much when it came to dad. Though when Kaleigh spoke about him, she could tell that it bothered him.

"If you ever want to come have dinner with Dad, just let me know and I can show you where and when to meet him." Kaleigh added, but Wesley stayed silent.

"Dad has some appointments coming up that I may need your help with. So many of his doctor's don't have late afternoon office hours." Kaleigh continued.

"I'll see what I can do. It is just so hard to leave the store mid-day." After this came more silence.

Kayleigh decided once more that it was best not to press the issue. Talking about the health problems of their father was not something Wesley seemed comfortable with. It was sad but the helpful, fun-loving brother-sister relationship had disappeared.

Growing up, while they had their differences, Kaleigh and Wesley, even during their busiest weeks, still found time to share secrets with each other as they hid in their treehouse in the backyard. Even when Kaleigh went off to college, they talked at least twice a week, filling each other in on what was happening in their lives. When Kaleigh had returned from college, their chats seemed to happen more in person at the Garden Center but still occasionally over the phone.

Looking back now, it was after Mom died that something began to change in Wesley. He grew more and more serious as the months went on. The conversations were fewer and were not as personal as they had once been. That night of the car crash that took their mother was a true blow to their family, and after that, things were never the same.

Then after Dad's fall and Kaleigh's time moving away from the family business, things between them had really shifted. The conversations turned from some form of connectedness to one of pure necessity, and Kaleigh wasn't sure why. It was like Wesley was burrowing into a shell. Wesley used to be one of the coolest kids in school, mixing kindness with fun humor and had such a great group of friends. They had a long-standing tradition of meeting at the diner for dinner and cards every Friday night. Throughout their years of growing up Kaleigh could confide in him. Even after Mom died, they had a few conversations about their feelings. She had to read his mood to know if he was up for one of these deeper conversations, but at least they happened. Whereas in the past, he was ready to talk anytime. Kaleigh was worried about her brother but figured that this change was probably due to the increased responsibility of the store, and the stress that came with the job.

Even in the conversation that night at Rita's, he wouldn't open up about anything. She had tried since then to begin conversations via text, asking how her brother was doing, and the replies varied. Sometimes he would answer with an "okay" and other times there was no reply. She always ended her messages to him with, "I'm here to talk anytime."

Kaleigh still wanted the chance to really talk with Wesley, to figure out what was wrong and how she could help. She would figure this out at some point.

Chapter 4

As Mrs. Wilson and Danielle slowly helped her into her desk chair, Kaleigh slowly reached for her phone, which had been on silent during her observation. She noticed three missed calls from Wesley, two missed calls from Havenwood, and three missed text messages.

She glanced at the messages. "Dad's gone" was the last text message that came in and the first one she read. Debbi had told her the news over the phone, that Dad had passed away, as Wesley had asked her to. But as she sat now, read the text and whispered the words, a huge wave of sadness washed over her, and chills ran over her body. Both Danielle and Mrs. Wilson heard the words Kaleigh whispered, put a hand on her shoulder, and said, "I'm so sorry."

At that moment, Mrs. Wilson turned to Danielle, asked her to help Kaleigh get to her car, and told her that she would find coverage for the last two periods of the day. Danielle packed up Kaleigh's work bag and helped her to her feet.

As Kaleigh walked down the hallway, she felt like everything was moving in slow motion, as if her head was in a fog. Thoughts of "I should've been there . . . I should have moved my observation and been there for Dad" ran through her head. Danielle said something, but she found it hard to hear what was being said. Finally, she heard, "Do you want me to drive you?" and turned her head to realize that it was Danielle.

"Umm, no, I can drive. I guess I will call Wes and find out where to go first. I'll be OK," Kaleigh said in what seemed like slow motion.

"OK, only if you're sure," Danielle checked one more time.

"Yes, I'll call you later. Thank you."

"If I don't hear from you by five o'clock, I'm calling you," Danielle replied.

"Thank you, friend," she said as they gave each other a hug.

****

Kaleigh spent the rest of the day talking to Wesley and then the doctor on-call at the hospital. Finally, she stopped and spoke with the staff at Havenwood. Her head was swirling, figuring out what happened and what needed to be done next, all the while making a mental list of what she needed to do. It turned out that Dad had passed away sometime after lunch. When the staff member went in to get him ready for his appointment, he couldn't wake him. CPR was started, and an ambulance was called, but it was too late. They said he was found lying on the couch in his room as if taking a nap, and was unresponsive.

Kaleigh's head continued to spin when she finally got home. The last thing she could remember was taking two pain relievers and flopping down on the bed. It had been a long, exhausting day.

When she woke up at 2:00 a.m., it took her a minute to figure out where she was and what day it was. She soon realized it was the day after her father had passed away. Her body was stiff as she tried to turn over and get comfortable so that she could fall back asleep, but that turned out to be impossible.

A few minutes later, Kaleigh decided to take a hot shower and put on fresh clothes. She hoped that this would help her relax so she could fall asleep. When she climbed under the covers, she peeked at her phone before setting it on the charger. She read all the text messages from yesterday for the first time. There was one from Dad's lead caregiver at Havenwood. It was a sweet one, saying how much she enjoyed her time taking care of him. There were three frantic messages from Wesley saying, "Where are you?" "Help, I don't know what to do," and the message she read earlier after falling into her desk chair at school saying, "Dad's gone."

Then there was a message from her principal, Mrs. Wilson, saying, "You really knocked it out of the park today, the best lesson I have seen in a long time! Don't worry about anything tomorrow. We have you covered. Call me Sunday if you can." And then, underneath all of those was a message from Jeremy. All it said was, "Missing you, Leigh."

Jeremy was her long-time friend from college. They had met sophomore year in chemistry class. He had helped her crawl through that class, and she managed to end the semester with a B. Science was always tough for Kaleigh, but Jeremy made everything manageable and better. There was never any spark between them, no romantic dates, no awkward feelings, just a wonderful friendship. They shared their deepest secrets, and they grew close. While away at college, many nights were spent at each other's place, not because anything was happening between them but because they enjoyed each other's company.

Jeremy lived a thousand miles away now and had a great career as a pharmacist at a health care center connected to a prestigious hospital. He and Kaleigh often texted each other, and when they were lucky enough to be available at the same time, they would catch up with a long phone call. She hadn't talked to him now in probably four months. This was the longest they had ever gone without talking. Life had been almost too much for Kaleigh lately. Looking back on these last few months, in the darkness of her bedroom, she wasn't sure how she had kept everything going.

She read Jeremy's text message again, smiled, sent him a caring emoji, a crying face, and a heart, placed her phone on the charger, turned off her alarm, and fell asleep.

****

At seven-thirty a.m., the ringing of her phone woke her up from a deep sleep. Startled, it took her a minute to realize that her phone was ringing. Her thoughts went to "Did I oversleep? What day is it?" Then she remembered Dad had passed away yesterday.

"Hello," she said in a groggy voice.

"Hi," said Jeremy. "You OK."

"Tryin' to be," she said after taking a sip of water from her glass on her bedside table, hoping to get rid of her groggy voice.

"What happened?" Jeremy said in his super caring voice.

After a pause, finding it hard to say the news aloud, she finally replied, "My dad died yesterday." This was the first time she had really spoken those words.

"Oh gosh, Leigh, I'm so sorry. What happened?" Jeremy and her dad were the only ones who called her by that name. Suddenly she felt a tear run down her cheek. Jeremy had met her dad a few times, and they got along very well. Ever since the first time they walked through the flower fields together that summer after her sophomore year, Jeremy had asked her if he could call her Leigh, like her dad. "You better check with my dad!" was Kaleigh's silly reply, but Jeremy obliged and asked her father. No one else had ever called her by that name but her father. Dad really liked Jeremy, and because he respected him, he told him, yes.

Kaleigh and Jeremy talked for over thirty minutes, and for the first time in a long time, she felt a slight sense of calm come over her. Jeremy had always been able to calm her. There was something about his voice and his caring nature that helped slow her breathing and slow her mind. She told him of these past few months when Dad's memory seemed to slip away more and more. She told of her daily visits to see him, even if just for fifteen minutes, to help keep their connection going. He had still remembered Kaleigh all this time, even though his long-term memory was almost gone. Then she spoke of Dad's caregiver, who had come into the room to get him ready for his doctor's appointment, finding him unresponsive. She shared how horrible it felt that she didn't move her observation, hadn't taken time off to be with her dad to take him to the appointment. She told him how she thought that maybe she could have prevented him dying yesterday, if she had only been there. She was upset with herself that she was not there to say goodbye, and immediately after saying this, Jeremy interrupted her.

"Leigh, you can't beat yourself up over this. You had a big appointment yourself, your observation. You have done so much for your dad since your mom's passing. There's nothing else you could have done."

After a quiet pause, she replied, "It would have been nice to be able to say goodbye." After she said these words, tears welled up in her eyes, and she couldn't make them stop.

"I know," Jeremy said softly, then noticed she was crying.

Without hesitation, he added, "I should come. Let me come and help you through all of this." Jeremy continued to hear her crying. He wished that he could reach through the phone and give her a hug.

"I know you are busy. My brother hasn't been much of a shoulder for me to lean on lately. I am not sure what is going on with him. We used to be close, but he has been so distant lately. I mean, we haven't really talked in so long. I have to find him today to start making plans for how we are all going to say goodbye."

Kaleigh's head began to swim again with all she had to do. To change the subject to something less heavy, she wiped her tears and said, "Oh gosh, I'm stealing the entire conversation. Tell me, what's new with you?" Kaleigh wanted to be there for her friend just as he was always there for her. She always enjoyed hearing about his life in the city, his job, and his sister Julia.

Jeremy told her of his job promotion, recently being named one of four managers in charge of the hospital-based pharmacy, including an increase in vacation time and pay. The real bonus was no longer having to work every weekend. His sister, whom Kaleigh bonded with over her visits to the city while she was in college, was now engaged to a great guy named Jacob. Jeremy told her how he loved her fiancé like he was his own brother, "Just a great guy," he said. You could just hear the happiness in his voice. His own mother had passed away around the time Kaleigh's mom did, which is part of the reason they continued to stay close even after college. They understood each other, cared for each other, and always knew what the other needed. Jeremy told of how his dad was traveling and still taking pictures for a national magazine. He shared how he always loved to travel and never seemed to want to settle down in one place for long, especially since his wife had passed away.

As the conversation wound down, Jeremy asked, "So when do you want me to come? And don't say I don't have to come. I'm coming. I have the vacation time; I just need to let my boss know."

"Let me figure a few things out today and text you tonight. I was thinking that Wednesday should be the Celebration of Life, but I have to check with Wes and the funeral home."

"OK," Jeremy replied, "but if you forget to text me, I will just make my own plans to come. Don't think that staying quiet will keep me at home. We need some good old-fashioned friend time! The only question is, pizza or barbecue?"

With that comment, Kaleigh chuckled and said, "Wow, Jeremy, have I missed you." Kaleigh's tears had dried, and she had even managed a smirk of a smile. Jeremy always knew how to make her feel better. "It will be so nice to see you. It's been so long."

"Too long," Jeremy replied. "See you soon."

"Thank you, friend," Kaleigh said as the call ended.

CHAPTER 5

After getting ready for the day and looking at all the piles in the kitchen, her phone rang again. It was Danielle calling to check in and see how her best friend was doing. As they hadn't been able to talk much last night, Danielle thought she would call during her free period. Kaleigh knew she needed help at that moment but hated to bother her friend with all of her mess.

Danielle was the kind of person who wouldn't take no for an answer and never complained, no matter how big the ask was. They had decided that Danielle would bring dinner over at 4:00 p.m., and they would work on whatever was needed for the grade book and future planning. They could share lesson plans so that Kaleigh's substitute would be ready without Kaleigh having to take hours and hours to prepare. Taking a week off as a teacher was almost not worth all the effort it took to prepare all of the plans for the absence.

Before then, Kaleigh would stop by the Garden Center and talk to Wesley; to the funeral home and talk to Kelly, one of the managers; and then to Havenwood to pick up Dad's special watch, his wallet, and his phone. Then there were so many calls to make. The overwhelming feeling that had settled in the pit of her stomach she was sure would be there for a while.

When she arrived at the Garden Center, Wesley was meeting with Teddy, most likely going through the punch list for the day, making notes of what was needed in the various departments and what orders were arriving when. Kaleigh gave a light wave so that Wesley knew she was here, then began straightening the register lanes, filling products from a cart that were left by the girl who was busy at the register. Kaleigh could never just stand still, especially now, with everything on her mind.

When Wesley was finally free, he came over to Kaleigh and said, "What's up?" as if nothing big had happened yesterday. He continued to seem so distant. And now was not the time to ask "What's wrong?"

"I just wanted your opinion on Dad's service. I was thinking of having a small, simple service on Wednesday at the funeral home with a light lunch at the Tavern afterward. The burial could be small and quiet, after lunch. I don't really want a lot of people at the cemetery, so maybe just close family and friends. What do you think?"

Wesley replied, "Sure, sounds good," as he nervously ran his fingers through his long hair and looked at the ground. Kaleigh noticed it had been a while since he cut it.

"Do you have any songs or verses you like? I mean, do you want to help me plan the service?" Kaleigh said to break the awkward silence.

"No." He paused, then said, "I'm sure whatever you and Kelly come up with will be fine. Just keep it short and sweet, I guess."

"Could you close the store on Wednesday so that you and the staff could be at the service and luncheon?" Kaleigh asked even though did not expect him to like that idea.

Wesley continued to be quiet. He pushed his hand through his hair again while he was thinking. "I guess we could close," he finally replied.

Just when Kaleigh thought there was nothing else to say, Wesley surprised her and said, "I guess I just never thought it would happen so soon." His eyes looked up for a minute and met Kaleigh's.

This was the first time Wesley had shared his feelings with her in a while. While it shocked her, at the same time she was grateful he had shared this with her. Maybe it was the first small step to really being able to talk again, share with each other like they used to.

After a moment Kaleigh replied, "I know."

Another quiet moment passed, then she said, "I'm sorry I couldn't go with Dad to his appointment. I should have changed things around so I could be there."

Wesley said nothing in reply. He eyes looked away and down at the ground once more.

She continued, "My phone was on silent during my observation, which is when you called and texted me."

There was another moment of silence, then finally, Wesley added to the conversation, "Yeah, I was wondering why you weren't answering your phone. I even did the emergency ring we used to do. You know, three rings, hang up, call again." Looking up for a moment his face showed a bit more color, and it was actually nice to be having a conversation with her brother.

After that thought ran through her mind, she continued, "I should call Dad's lawyer too. There must be paperwork to fill out, a will to—"

Wesley quickly interrupted, "I can call Dan. I'll take care of that." Then, suddenly, continuing to rush his words, he said, "I have to go. I will have Theresa make the signs for our closure. Just let me know the times of the events. I'll call the lawyer. Sorry I have to go. We are just so busy here." And just like that, he was walking away.

"Oh, Wes," she called after him, and he stopped. "I still have the greenhouse lease that Dad wanted me to look at. You know, renting from Mr. Thomas' farm."

After a pause, Wesley stopped and said, "OK, just bring it by, and Teddy and I will look at it." And in a flash, he was gone. She was hopeful because the first part of their conversation went well but thought it odd that as soon as she mentioned the lawyer, Wesley began rushing his words and wanting to leave. This thought left her mind when she remembered that she needed to get to the funeral home, and she turned and walked back toward the entrance doors.

Just as her hand was on the door, she saw Jackson on the other side of the glass. He was pulling a wagon with crates of vegetables, bringing fresh produce for a busy Friday morning.

"Oh, hi, Jackson," Kaleigh said as he held the door open for her.

"I heard about your father. I'm so sorry." Jackson leaned in to give her a hug, holding her for just longer than a normal hug, during which she replied, "Thank you."

As Jackson pulled away, he asked, "Is there anything I can do? I really want to help you and Wes." Jackson had his complete focus on Kaleigh, not trying to even pull his wagon into the building yet even though he was running a few minutes late this morning. They stood outside and continued their conversation.

"I'm on my way to the funeral home now and then the Tavern, so I will let you know afterward." Kaleigh sighed as she felt the stress of everything pressing deeper onto her shoulders.

"Wes isn't coming with you?" Jackson asked in a surprised tone.

"No, you know he is busy. I asked him yesterday if he would come, but he said he couldn't. I just stopped by this morning to ask if he had any special requests for the service. He didn't offer any help or suggestions. He probably just wants to keep his week as normal as possible, I guess. You know, we all grieve in our own way. He did say that he would contact our lawyer and financial guy, Dan."

"Do you want some company today?" Jackson asked in his soft, caring voice.

"No, I'll be OK. But thank you for offering." Kaleigh was touched by his offer. And somehow, she knew he would drop everything if she said yes.

"And how are you?" Jackson said as he put a hand on her arm.

"I am stressed and tired but trying to focus on one thing at a time. If I think of everything all at once, I will end up overwhelmed, and then I'll be no good for anything." Just then, she took a quick peek at her phone and realized she was going to be late if she didn't leave now. "Oh, I have to go."

"Wait," Jackson said with a pause as he grabbed her hand. Kaleigh stopped and thought she felt her heart skip a beat. "Meet me for a drink tomorrow. You pick the time and place, and I won't take no for an answer," he said with a sly smile.

Kaleigh couldn't say no to that smile. She found herself cracking a little smile herself as she replied, "Sure, two o'clock, Rita's?"

"Sounds perfect," Jackson replied.

CHAPTER 6

The summer when Dad fell, Kaleigh worked tirelessly to help her brother at the store. There were quite a few nights when Jackson would come to the store at closing time. He was pretending to check on his produce but really was looking for a chance to catch Kaleigh. He enjoyed talking to her and often asked if he could take her for a drink. Most of the time, she agreed, and they went out together, either to the Mexican restaurant, Rita's bar, or to the park to find a food truck and walk around.

One summer night, they decided to eat at the Mexican restaurant instead of just having a drink at the bar. Kaleigh had missed lunch due to a big mix-up with a delivery, which meant she had to completely rethink the main window display.

Their conversations were always meaningful, talking about growing up in Forest Grove, their family, friends, and relationships. Neither one of them had ever been super serious about anyone, but they had known each other for so long that they could confide in each other and share things that they often couldn't with their own siblings. On that night, the conversation included friends from high school, Hailey and Ethan, who were never friends in school but, in the past year, had found themselves dating each other and were suddenly engaged. No one saw that match coming, and the two were happy for them. Ethan was a landscaper who often came into the Garden Center to place orders for clients, and Hailey was in medical billing or something to that effect. Both came from two different worlds, but both seemed like a good match for one another, and Kaleigh and Jackson could see that relationship working out.

After dinner, they walked through the park, which was lit with twinkle lights in preparation for the upcoming festival. After having a large margarita and feeling tired, Kaleigh found herself holding Jackson's hand as they followed the path through the trees. They talked about what they imagined being in love could be like and what they each hoped for in a future partner. There was no spark between them that Kaleigh could feel, but for Jackson, it was different. Jackson had been growing more and more fond of Kaleigh as the weeks and months went by.

Later that night, Jackson drove Kaleigh home, and she invited him in to watch the new detective show that was starting in ten minutes. They sat together on the couch, and before she knew it, she had fallen asleep, her head on his shoulder, dreaming peacefully. Jackson let her head rest on him for over an hour, then rested her head on a pillow, covered her with a blanket, and left her a sweet note that read, "I had a wonderful time tonight. The conversation and your friendship is amazing." He even added a heart and a smiley face at the end. 😊

That was the first night and the last for a long time that Jackson ended up coming into Kaleigh's house—not because the company wasn't great but because life was busy. The summer after that one, Kaleigh began traveling again and was not at the Garden Center quite as much. She spent more time with Danielle as their friendship grew stronger in their second school year, and they had planned a long vacation together. Their road trip lasted almost three weeks and was just what they needed to celebrate another successful school year.

When she returned, it was getting close to Hailey and Ethan's wedding. About two weeks before the event, Jackson finally caught up with Kaleigh at the Garden Center. He had been trying to find her for a couple of weeks now, but she and Danielle had been on their trip. Jackson never liked to call people on the phone. He typically only used his cell phone for occasional work calls and emergencies. Anything he needed to talk to anyone about, he would rather find them in person.

"Hey, stranger!" Jackson came up from behind and startled Kaleigh as she was setting out new flowers. She immediately smiled and laughed, and she quickly found herself embraced in a hug.

"Oh my gosh, I haven't seen you in so long!" Jackson's hug was always warm.

Before he could lose the nerve, he asked, "Did you get an invitation to Ethan and Hailey's wedding?"

"Yes, I did. I actually found a dress while I was on vacation last week."

Jackson hesitated for a few seconds as the voice inside his head said, *Just ask her already!* "Would you be my date . . . to the wedding?" Jackson spoke in a shy voice as he was worried she would say no.

"Of course," Kaleigh replied, and Jackson tried to hold back his sigh of relief so she wouldn't know how nervous he was. "Awesome" was all he could muster, and he immediately regretted his choice of words.

"You free for a drink later?" he added.

"I can't go tonight, but let's meet for coffee tomorrow," she replied. He was disappointed but took the invite for the next day as a win.

At the coffee shop, they talked about the particulars of the wedding. They decided to purchase a gift together, ordered it online, and had it delivered to Kaleigh's house. Once they figured out the gift, she shared memories of the fun she and Danielle had on vacation. They had rented a small house by the beach and just relaxed. Each morning they woke up and just let the day take them where it may. The two did not make any plans and did not let anything bring them stress, but instead focused on living in the moment. Kaleigh's favorite night was when they ate outdoors at a Mexican restaurant and then walked the beach after dark. The ocean breeze, the lights, and the music were perfect, and she felt herself not wanting to leave. As she spoke, Jackson could picture her walking on the beach with the wind in her hair, and found himself smiling.

Jackson filled her in on his family. He spoke of the continued success of his produce sales at the Garden Center and thanked Kaleigh for taking a chance on him. Then he shared his sister's semester abroad in London. She was studying fashion design and had dreams of opening her own clothing store someday. He told Kaleigh that the last time Kathryn talked to him she had called her future store a boutique. Jackson laughed when he said the word. It just seemed like a weird word for him to say.

Jackson's parents were older and had retired from farm life a few years back. They were living in his grandparents' house just outside of town. They lived a simple life and were proud of Jackson for taking over the family farm and increasing business. He was grateful to Kaleigh for giving him the chance to sell produce at her father's store. He was proud that he was improving on the business his parents had left him, and loved that the addition of his business at the Garden Center was the first stepping stone in growing his families legacy.

Kaleigh and Jackson's conversation always picked up as if no time had passed. Even though it had been almost two months since they had talked, they could always talk freely as if no time had passed at all. The more time Jackson spent with Kaleigh, the deeper his feelings for her grew. He was beginning to picture her in his life, not just as a friend, but as his person. He pictured a life with her, and in his dreams, it was amazing.

CHAPTER 7

The afternoon of the wedding was sweet. The weather was perfect—sunny but not too hot. Kaleigh wore a simple lavender dress with her hair swept up and tendrils hanging down. Danielle had helped her pick out a bangle bracelet with shells on it and small hoop earrings from a shop they had found as they explored the town by the beach.

Jackson arrived at her door dressed in a suit and tie, looking very handsome with a cleanly shaven face and some gel in his hair. Kaleigh was pleasantly surprised. She had never seen him like this before. What also surprised her was that he was carrying a jewelry box.

As Jackson stepped into her entryway he held out the box wrapped with a flower corsage wristlet, and placed it in her hand.

"What is this?" Kaleigh finally got the words out as she felt like her mouth all of a sudden turned dry.

"Just a little something." He smiled, still holding a hand under hers.

"This is not little," she added.

He couldn't stop smiling as he took the corsage off of the box and put it on her wrist. As he watched her open the gold box, Kaleigh, trying to keep her mouth from dropping open, saw the small silver open heart with one beautiful, sparkling diamond at its tip. It was perfect, not overdone, or too big, just beautiful. A tear came to her eye as she realized no one had ever given her a gift this special before. This was completely too much, unexpected, and amazing. She still couldn't find the words. It was as if she had so much to say, yet she couldn't speak.

Just then, Jackson took the necklace slowly out of the box and put it around Kaleigh's neck. As this happened, she stared into the hallway mirror, just watching in amazement. Finally, she managed to say in a small, quiet voice, "Jackson, thank you. I don't know what to say. It's . . . it's beautiful!"

"So are you!" Jackson quickly replied as he gave her a kiss on her cheek.

As she looked in the mirror, touching the necklace gently with her fingers her quiet voice asked, "Why such a beautiful gift?"

"Ask me again later. We should get going. Do you have the gift?"

"Oh, yes, you got me so flustered I would have forgotten it," Kaleigh said as she grabbed her shawl and her small handbag with her cell phone and some lip gloss in it. She never used much makeup, believing that simplicity was better. She turned toward the kitchen island to get the large wrapped box, but he beat her to it, saying, "I'll get it."

The evening was amazing. Spending time with one of her best friends on a beautiful farm on a perfect summer evening, complete with a stunning barn lit with a zillion twinkle lights, was like something out of a storybook. Hailey and Ethan were the perfect couple, and everything about the day was just stunning.

When the reception was winding down, Jackson asked Kaleigh if she would like to take a walk. The path to the garden gazebo by the small lake was lit with bright solar lights. The sun was beginning to set, and the colors of the sky looked like a painting. Jackson held her hand as the two walked slowly down the lit path toward the gazebo.

When they got there, they sat down next to each other. Kaleigh found herself looking at the beautiful lake, which was as smooth as glass and showed the reflection of the sunset in the water. All the while, Jackson was looking at her. After a few quiet moments passed, he whispered, "Ask me again."

Her mind was so relaxed that without thinking, she replied, "What?"

"Ask me the question you asked when I gave you the necklace," he reminded her.

"Oh," she tried to keep her breathing slow, but it was an impossible task. She didn't know why she was suddenly nervous but her once calm heart began to race. She turned to him as he grabbed both of her hands.

Trying not to stutter in nervousness, she asked, "Why such a beautiful gift?"

Jackson was nervous as well. His heart seemed to be beating out of his chest. He took a deep breath and began what he had practiced in his mind a million times over.

"I am in love with you." He finally got the words out, then continued before she could say anything. "I wake up every morning and you are the first thing I think about. I come by the Garden Center more often than I should, just to see you, even if just for a couple of minutes. The conversations we have, the laughs that we share, I want that. I want you in my life every day." He stopped in his tracks, and suddenly, the only thing he could hear was his heart trying to jump out of his chest.

Kaleigh, whose head was swimming at this moment, didn't know what to say. She looked into his eyes the entire time he was speaking to her, and she could feel her heart sinking in her chest. In the hours since he had given her the necklace she had in the back of her mind that maybe this meant he wanted more than a casual friendship, but love, wow. She had never been in love before and didn't know how she would feel when she realized she was. All she knew was what she saw in movies. She had never thought of Jackson in that way and wasn't sure she felt love for him—that true kind of love when you were sure you had met *your* person. The feeling of butterflies every time you saw him, were with him – she had heard of people having that reaction but it wasn't anything she had ever felt. She had always thought of Jackson more like a brother, never as a lover.

Too much time had gone by now, and Jackson was getting more nervous. He finally managed to get the words "Say something" kindly and softly out of his mouth.

Kaleigh looked toward the lake for a moment, then turned to him and said, "Jackson, you know your friendship means the world to me." Jackson's heart sank in his chest, and his throat became dry. This whole time he was hoping Kaleigh felt the same way, but with this reaction, he realized that his dream was not going to become a reality.

Kaleigh continued, "I have missed our talks, our walks through the park. Life has just been different, busy, lately. I have always thought of you as a best friend, a big brother. And with Wesley and my relationship changing, I have found myself confiding in you more, and you have truly been there for me. I appreciate you so much. You have been a shoulder to lean on and I cherish what we have. I'm sorry I haven't been around much lately, but I'm so sorry." The silence in this moment seemed like an eternity. "I don't want this to ruin our friendship but," and there it was, "I just don't think I feel the same way."

There was nothing left to say. The two sat in that gazebo in silence for what seemed like close to ten minutes. At one point, Kaleigh put a hand on his shoulder and said, "Can I?" as if to ask if she could still put her head on his shoulder. "Sure," he replied in a quiet voice as he put his arm around her. Then Kaleigh quietly whispered, "I'm sorry. I just hope this doesn't change things between us." Jackson let out a disappointed sigh. They sat in silence for about ten more minutes, then agreed it was time to go.

When Jackson pulled up to Kaleigh's house, he put the car in park and left it running. He was too devastated to be a gentleman and go around to open her door as he did when he picked her up just hours before. Kaleigh looked at him and said once again, "I'm sorry, I'm so sorry," then reached over to give him a hug. He held her there, wishing so hard that things would have turned out differently. "Can we still be friends?" she dared to ask. And without hesitation, he said, "Yes." While he was devastated that she was not going to be his, he could not imagine a life without her either. Then, he watched her walk inside before driving away.

It was a month that went by before Jackson could build up the courage to find Kaleigh at the Garden Center and ask her to go with him for a drink, like old times. And for the next couple of years, Kaleigh worked hard to do her part to keep the friendship and the connection going. There were times when she would go to visit him at his farm and invite him out for a bite to eat, so he knew that the friendship went both ways. She felt so terrible that she had let him down like that. In all the ways she imagined love, it was more than what she felt for Jackson, but she could not imagine her life without him.

That was two years ago.

CHAPTER 8

The funeral home visit went as well as could be expected. Kelly, one of the managers there, had known Dad for many years. Dad always sent the prettiest flowers to decorate her office, and she would visit Dad from time to time and bring him some of her famous sweet treats. Kelly's amazing baked goods were known all over Forest Grove.

Kelly had asked Kaleigh if they had contacted Dad's attorney, who may have information on what should be done after Dad's passing. She also mentioned asking about a life insurance policy that might help to pay for expenses this week. Kaleigh told her that Wesley had decided to take care of that. Dad never talked about what would happen when he passed away, but being that her father was such an organized person, there had to be something written down. She quickly set a reminder on her phone to call Wesley on Sunday and ask if he had contacted Dan at the lawyer's office.

By the time Kaleigh left the funeral home, the service was planned, thanks to Kelly's beautiful ideas. After that, she had stopped by the Tavern, booked the event space, and planned the menu. The manager said he would take care of ordering the dessert, paired with some of Kelly's amazing treats, which were some of Dad's favorites. The burial would follow the luncheon, with only immediate family and friends invited. Kelly and Kaleigh had worked on the list and designed the postcard, which would quietly be handed out after the funeral only to those who needed the information. Kelly would see that everything would be taken care of. Thank goodness, she was there and knew her dad so well.

Kaleigh, alone at this moment, needed Kelly's guidance and compassion. Of course, she would have rather had Wesley with her, but then again, it wasn't like they were as close as they used to be, or that he wanted to be a part of any of these decisions. Maybe they would have just disagreed on everything, which would have made going through this sadness, this planning, even worse. Or, he would have sat there, not saying anything, which would have annoyed her. Kelly was impartial, knew her dad, and knew what he would have wanted. She had made this dreaded day not so horrible.

At this point, it was past three o'clock, and she was emotionally exhausted. She decided to stop at the grocery store and pick up some fun food items to make a quick charcuterie board with a couple of choices of wine. While Danielle was bringing dinner, Kaleigh did not want to be the kind of host who had absolutely nothing in the refrigerator. She even splurged and bought fresh-ground coffee.

Danielle came in with dinner from the new sandwich place that had opened next to the diner in town. Everyone was raving about it at school, but the two had not tried it yet. There were choices of a small sub sandwich or a couple of different kinds of wraps. She had made sure to grab a couple of small bags of their favorite chips and a clear fizzy drink, as she figured Kaleigh's stomach might need a little settling, just as it did that night after Ethan and Hailey's wedding. She thought back to the time when Kaleigh reached out in an SOS call to Danielle the moment Jackson had dropped her off the night of the wedding. The night Jackson professed his love to her and Kaleigh had let him down. Danielle always knew what Kaleigh needed, and she always told herself that one day, her friend would be there for her when the tables were turned. However, lately it was always Kaleigh who needed saving.

The two teachers began with the cheese-and-fruit platter while Kaleigh updated her friend on the events of the day, including the part about Jackson wanting to go for coffee tomorrow. Kaleigh quickly grabbed her phone and set a reminder, just in case she forgot amidst everything else going on.

Danielle stopped Kaleigh at the part about the attorney and asked her why she thought Wesley had begun speaking so quickly the moment she brought that up. After thinking for a moment, she decided that maybe Wesley was just feeling overwhelmed about everything and that these big decisions and impending discussions with an attorney could very well get a person's heart racing.

Within two hours, the girls had checked and replied to every email and put in for a substitute for Kaleigh for the week, and Danielle had shared what she had begun for her English 7 and English 8 lesson plans. The two taught the same curriculum, so sharing was easy. They kept things simple for the week, as their eighth grade students were working on writing their own stories and doing planning sheets for each element before beginning their rough draft. Kaleigh's slideshow on character creation was a hit with the students, so they decided to expand it to include tips on figuring out the best setting, problem, and solution to help students craft more engaging stories. The students had the worksheets already copied in their packets, so the plans came together quite easily. Their seventh graders were reading a new story, so the two teachers wrote plans to kick off the story and begin the process of journaling and student literature circles for each chapter.

The last thing to tackle was the piles of papers that needed to be graded and put into the report card system. After a thirty-minute break to talk about Danielle and what was going on with her family, they quickly organized the piles and divided and conquered the grading. Kaleigh could not have been more thankful for her friend saving the day once again. By the time Danielle left, there were just three piles of graded papers left to be inputted into the computer, which Kaleigh hoped to complete tomorrow, after her coffee with Jackson. She would also get the bills paid so that the last of the piles could disappear, and her kitchen would once again look like a kitchen. She had not felt this organized in a long time and was determined to finish tomorrow, no matter what. The paperwork for the lease of the greenhouse, well, maybe she would bring that to the Garden Center on Sunday. That would give her an excuse to go and talk to Wesley.

****

The next morning, Kaleigh was up and making breakfast before nine. She had tried to stay in bed longer, but her slight headache was calling for a cup of coffee. She had not made herself eggs in a long time and was thankful she had thought to buy a dozen when she was at the store yesterday.

She had a lot of nervous energy this morning, maybe due to the list of things she needed to do that were swimming in her head. While her eggs began to cook, she decided to write her list down on paper. Maybe this would help her focus on one thing at a time and calm her down. Getting too many thoughts running through her head at one time would just overwhelm her, and then she would not be as productive. She was missing her father, and for some reason she was a bit nervous about her visit with Jackson. Ever since the day of Ethan and Hailey's wedding, she found herself a bit nervous just before their meeting. After all this time she still felt bad to have turned him down, though she knew it was the right thing to do. No one wants a person who pretends to be something they are not—in this case, pretending to be in love with a person when the feelings aren't there.

Kaleigh ended up cleaning the entire house and paying all the bills before her alarm went off to remind her about her coffee date that wasn't a date. She had just enough time to shower and get ready before needing to leave for the coffee shop. She couldn't remember the last time she had an entire morning to do what was on her list, what she needed to do, and it felt good.

Jackson was wearing his denim jacket with khaki pants and his amazing smile. His hair was a bit longer, a dirty blond with long tendrils combed to the side. He waited for her in his truck, and when he saw her pull into the lot, he got out and walked toward the porch to meet her. They smiled as they walked toward each other, and when Kaleigh came up to him, he gently opened his arms, and she came and tucked herself inside them. It took less than five seconds for the tears to begin to fall. She had kept the sadness in as long as she could, but something about Jackson's embrace had caused her emotions to tumble.

In amazing Jackson fashion, he knew just what to do. He stroked her long hair, gently rubbed her back, and said, "I'm here for you. I'll always be here." It was exactly what she needed. Since Dad passed away, Wesley had been even more distant, barely returning any text messages with much more than an "OK." Kaleigh had texted him the times for the service and the luncheon afterward and asked him one more time if he had a special song or verse he particularly liked, and to that question there was no reply. Kaleigh had been entirely alone in this and had tried so hard to keep it together, but her emotions were no match for Jackson's arms.

It took a few moments for Kaleigh to gather herself and stop the tears from falling. As they walked into the coffee shop, Jackson went up to the counter and brought back a napkin for her to dry her eyes. He had known just what she needed. Then he ordered her a warm cup of coffee while she chose a seat and tried to get herself together. Their conversation lasted over two hours. Kaleigh shared everything that had been going on, including all the plans that had been made and all the help Danielle had given her. She talked about all the work she had been able to accomplish this morning after not being able to put her complete focus on what she needed to do for so long. She also mentioned how she felt like she might just be able to finish her grading this evening and actually see her kitchen counters by the end of the night.

Then they talked about Wesley. There was just so much to say. They had been so close, but during these years of transition, after mom died, and Dad wasn't able to work as much at the Garden Center, things began to change. Then when Dad's health took even more of a turn, Kaleigh had to pull completely away from the family business, the two grew even more distant. Kaleigh could not pinpoint any argument, any disagreement, or anything that she may have done wrong, just that she was not available to help him anymore at the store.

Jackson listened for the longest time as Kaleigh poured her heart out in front of him. When she finally took a breath and rested her voice, she said, "I'm so sorry, I've been rambling."

"No, don't apologize. That is what I'm here for. You are going through so much and having to do everything on your own. I just want you to know that I am still here for you." At this moment Jackson paused, looked down at his coffee and added. "I realize that I made a fool of myself all those years ago—"

And in that second, Kaleigh interrupted him. "No, Jackson, please don't think of that night as making a fool of yourself. I don't think of you as a fool at all. If anything, it was me who felt awful, like I was letting you down." This was the most they had ever spoken of that night. And just then, Jackson put his hand on top of hers and said, "Looking back on it now, I realize that it wouldn't have been a good idea to start a relationship when we both weren't feeling the same way. It took me this long to be able to say that, but I want you to know that I will always care deeply for you, and I still want to be in your life, to help you in any way that I can."

"Thank you, Jackson," she said as she put her hand on top of his and looked into his eyes. Maybe it was that her emotions were heightened, but she swore she felt a butterfly in her stomach and a warmth in her heart at that moment. In her mind ran the thoughts of how Jackson was such an amazing person, and that she was so incredibly lucky to have him in her life. "Thank you so much," she added, squeezing his hand.

After a quiet moment had passed, she wanted to turn the conversation away from her and on to her best friend. "So, what is going on in your life lately?" Jackson smiled and told her a little bit about the success at the farm with Laney, his cousin, beginning to take on more responsibility. She had offered to run the roadside farm stand and how she was using her artistic talent to create signs and sell more produce. He also told how she began a special of the day to entice customers to come back more often.

Laney had graduated high school and was taking part-time art classes at the local community college while she was figuring out her path in life. Kaleigh loved how Jackson spoke of her "figuring out her path." Wasn't that what everyone in life was doing, day after day, finding out what path they were on or which path they should take, wondering if they were on the right one? Kaleigh had found her path in career, but never in love. Who knows, she thought, maybe someday the path to love and her happiness would become clear.

Before they knew it, two hours had passed by. Kaleigh needed to get back home to discover what to have for dinner and get back to her grading. Jackson walked Kaleigh to her car and said goodbye. He knew what her plan was for the rest of the evening and immediately knew what he would do.

Back at home, Kaleigh had gotten out the rest of the cheese and grapes from her refrigerator and was content with that as her dinner. She had not been home for more than twenty-five minutes when the doorbell rang. It was Jackson with her favorite pizza from Pizza Palace. She laughed as she remembered all those years ago when they would grab pizza with Wesley and his friend Kayla occasionally after school. It was a great inexpensive option when they were all broke, but oh, it was delicious! Even to this day, the sauce made this pizza taste like home.

Kaleigh let him in and followed him to the kitchen, where a few pieces of cheese and some grapes sat on the counter. "Is this your idea of dinner?" he asked.

"Not anymore!" she said with a smile and a laugh, taking the pizza box from his hands and setting it on the island counter. Jackson watched as she twisted her hair into a bun before opening the box of delicious comfort food. Kaleigh didn't realize he was watching her. He always felt that she was the most beautiful woman, and he was happy to spend time with her, even if she wasn't his.

"I don't want to keep you from your work," he quickly moved the conversation along.

"Nonsense. I mean, if you don't mind me typing while we eat, you are welcome to stay. I just want these piles gone. I have a feeling there is more to do this week than I realize." She grabbed plates out of the cupboard and asked him if he would rather have wine or beer and poured them each a drink.

They talked and laughed for hours while Kaleigh put her grades into the computer. There were stories of animals on Jackson's farm that left their pens and got away and a rooster that was trying to boss around a cow, trying to make him go where she wanted him to, and the two were laughing. Then there was the story of Jackson's sister trying her hand at fixing their parents front porch and ending up falling through it. After returning from a semester in London, she was determined to help fix up the house a bit. One afternoon she had called Jackson in hysteria, confusing him as to whether she was hurt or not. He could not tell whether she was laughing or crying on the phone. He raced over there quickly only to find her laughing in her funny snorting way, with her body half above the porch and half under it. Needless to say, Jackson sent over his carpenter friend to finish the job and save the day. That story fit Jackson's sister to a tee! Apparently, her time in London had not given her any carpentry skills! Kaleigh mentioned that maybe she should keep her plan to become a fashion designer. They both agreed that career suited her much better than a DIYer!

Once the papers were finished, Kaleigh put them into two bags and put them in her car to be returned to school at a later date. She came back in and felt so accomplished. "I am proud of me," she said as she took her seat at the island and had another sip of her wine. Without hesitation, Jackson agreed, saying, "I am proud of you too!" Then he asked, "Hey, are you up for watching our detective show?" To which Kaleigh replied, "Absolutely, I'll meet you in the den."

Kaleigh wanted to get out of her jeans but didn't want her pajamas on yet, so she chose her lavender sweater and leggings. She wanted to relax with her best friend and looked forward to watching their show as they used to. There was something comforting about this. This time, Kaleigh made it through most of the show before falling asleep. As she was closing her eyes, her head on his shoulder, she remembered whispering, "Can you stay?" and without hesitation, he answered, "Yes."

Chapter 9

It was on the cold, rainy nights in Forest Grove when Kaleigh felt most alone. Seven years ago on a cold stormy night was when she lost her mom in a tragic car accident. And since her death, she would imagine her mom driving in that rainstorm, her car slipping off the road, and slamming into a tree. The police officer had told them in detail what had happened, and she pictured the tragedy over and over in her head for weeks. Kaleigh had wanted to know every detail of the accident, even though it was painful.

Within five months of the accident, the visual replay of the accident crept into her dreams. On every stormy night since, Kaleigh would have that nightmare, reliving what happened the night her mother died, and it would wake her up out of a deep sleep, scaring her and making her heart race. She had told Jackson so many things in all of their conversations, but never about the nightmares.

And tonight, an hour after they had both fallen asleep on the couch, the rain and thunder had moved in. As the two slept next to each other on the couch, Kaleigh had the dream, waking up just as the car crashed into the tree. Startled, just like every stormy night, she suddenly found herself sitting upright and breathing heavily. Jackson was completely startled and scared, and once he realized what was going on, he rubbed Kaleigh's back and used his calming voice to settle her nerves. When she had calmed down, she found herself jumping into his arms and sobbing.

About three minutes later, she pulled away, wiped her tears, and got up to get herself a glass of water. Jackson was completely worried about his best friend but didn't know how much he should pry. He decided to give her space and wait for her to speak. When she returned, she looked right into his eyes and said, "I'm sorry," as she knew that she had scared him.

"What are you apologizing for?" Jackson quickly replied. "I am just glad I was here to help you. Has this happened to you before?"

"Yes, on these stormy nights, they bring back the memories of the night of my mom's death, the horrible car crash, into my dreams. My brain goes right back to replaying that terrible accident, and the minute the car hits the tree, I awake, scared, my heart racing." Kaleigh wasn't sure how he would react to her story. The room was quiet for a few moments as she sipped her water. Then, as if water was about to fall off a cliff, she poured everything out to her best friend. As she poured her heart and her feelings out to Jackson, all he could think about was how he was so glad he was here to help her. He was grateful that she had asked him to stay, that he was here for her when she needed him.

When she had finished her story, all he could say was "I'm so sorry, Kaleigh. I wish I could help you through this." Then, without even thinking, he added, "How long after one of these dreams does it take you to fall back to sleep?"

"It depends, but usually once I have some water and relax my breathing, I can get back to sleep okay." Kaleigh replied, taking another sip of water.

"Do you want me to stay?" He asked.

And in that moment, she stood up, wiped a tear from her cheek, held out her hand, and led him slowly to her bedroom. They did not say another word, but they crawled into bed, not as lovers, but as friends. Jackson stayed on his side of the bed but reached a hand out to hold hers. She squeezed his hand, said, "Thank you," and closed her eyes. She found herself listening to Jackson's breathing, feeling a calmness and warmth come over her. And, for the first time in a long time, she felt safe.

****

The next morning, she awoke late, as she had forgotten to set her alarm, let alone charge her phone. She heard the sound of her front door closing, and before she knew it, Jackson was entering her bedroom with fresh coffee and breakfast from the diner. Breakfast in bed was something Kaleigh had never had a day in her life. Just then, she became nervous about her hair and what she must look like, and she started reaching up to fix her bun.

Just then Jackson entered the room. "Don't . . ." He paused, and she stopped fussing. "You look beautiful." All she could do was smile.

"I can't thank you enough for staying with me last night. I'm sorry if I scared you." Kaleigh blushed a little as she said the words.

"I am so glad I was here for you. I can't imagine you going through this at night all alone." And just then, he paused. He wasn't sure if what he was going to say next was going to upset her. For a moment, he just looked at her. When she realized that he was staring at her, she said, "What? You can tell me." And to that, Jackson replied, "Do you think you should talk to someone? I mean, maybe talking to a counselor will help ease your dreams. I would hate to have you suffer with these bad dreams on every stormy night forever."

The room got quiet as Kaleigh thought carefully of what to say. She was determined not to hurt his feelings anymore. He did have a good point, although she wasn't sure that therapy would solve her problem. Finally, she replied, "Yes, that probably isn't a bad idea. It would be nice not to have these nightmares anymore."

"You know I am always here for you, but I mean, someone with a degree in this stuff might have better luck in the desired outcome . . . to get rid of these dreams." And as he finished the words, he bent over to kiss her cheek and said goodbye.

"Thank you, Jackson," she said. "Thank you for everything."

"There's no friend I'd rather be with." He smiled and closed the door behind him.

****

Later that afternoon, when Kaleigh went to the Garden Center, she brought the lease offer for the greenhouse. It was from the neighboring farm, and they were holding the greenhouse for dad so he would be able to grow more for the store, especially through the colder months. Kaleigh and Dad were supposed to review it together, but his memory these last months made it difficult to have any conversations with him, especially regarding the Garden Center.

She had texted Wesley that she needed to talk to him today and that she would be at the center at 9:30 a.m. She wanted to make sure to have time with him before the store opened.

When she arrived, Wesley was running around as usual, writing notes on his clipboard and filling carts with stock that needed to go out today. His first crew would be starting their shifts in thirty minutes.

"Hey, Wes, can we talk for a minute, no distractions?"

After a moment, he paused, set down his pen, and replied, "Sure."

"I have the greenhouse lease," she began. "A few months back, on one of Dad's better days, he seemed to want to go ahead with the lease. You know he was so disappointed that he lost so much of the crop from the field with last winter's colder temperatures lasting longer than expected. I know he thought it was a great way to ensure some amazing flowers each year, no matter the weather. I think Dad would want you to go ahead with it."

"Yeah, I will talk to Terry, but you are probably right." Wesley seemed agreeable and calm, a tone she had not heard in a long time.

"You know you could plant much earlier, too, in the greenhouse. I talked to the owners about it a month ago, and they were still holding it for us." Kaleigh added.

"For us?" Wesley replied. And there it was. The resentment in his voice told Kaleigh that he was upset with her for not being able to help anymore.

"Are you upset with me?" Kaleigh tried to keep her voice calm.

"I have always needed help running this place. First I lost Dad, then you. It's just been a lot." Wesley got quiet and ran his fingers nervously through his hair. His voice seemed full of frustration.

"I'm sorry, Wes. You know that I have given so much of my time to this place, but when Dad took a turn and needed more help, there wasn't any extra time. And when the house needed selling, I just could not fit it in. I thought you would understand." Kaleigh was trying her best to stay calm and not turn defensive.

"It is a lot, and I never expected all of this to be on my shoulders, and so soon. I have no life except this store, and I . . ." Wesley trailed off in his thoughts.

After a moment of Wesley staying quiet Kaleigh began, "You knew I wasn't going to take over this store when I got my teaching degree. It didn't . . . it doesn't have to be all you. We can get you—" And just then, Wesley cut her off just as she was going to say the word "help."

"I can't talk about this right now. What else do you need?" Kaleigh noticed that his voice was turning more harsh. All the while she was keeping hers surprisingly calm.

"You got my texts about Wednesday's service and events?" she asked.

"Yes," he said bluntly.

"Kelly is sending over the flyers for you to get to the staff, and we are making postcards for the close family and friends that we want to invite to the cemetery after lunch." Kaleigh continued.

"OK" was all Wesley could muster.

"Can you pick out the suit you would like Dad to wear and bring it to the funeral home by tomorrow?" she asked. It was the only task she had left to give him short of making an appointment with the lawyer.

"There were a couple of suits in the back of his closet at Havenwood." She added, in case he was not sure where to get Dad's suit from.

"I don't think I'll have time," Wesley said after a slight pause.

Now Kaleigh's voice finally sounded annoyed. She couldn't believe his response. "Really Wes? You really want no part of the service preparation?" Kaleigh didn't like the anger she was beginning to feel inside.

"I just can't" was all he could say.

"Can you at least make an appointment for us to meet with the lawyer to figure out the next steps and whether he has a life insurance policy to help pay expenses?" Kaleigh had no idea what would he would say to this final request.

"Yeah, sure, I have inventory this week, but I'll do it. I need to go now." His voice was harsh and fast as he picked up the greenhouse lease and his clipboard and walked away.

"Let me know about the lawyer. Bye, I guess," Kaleigh sighed as her brother disappeared, walking back toward the office.

Kaleigh didn't know what to do next. She was completely frustrated with her brother. She took some deep breathes in the fresh air to help her calm down. The sun felt warm as she sat in her car, but the breeze outside was chilly. She hadn't dressed for this cool breeze today. She texted Jackson about Wesley not wanting to pick out the suit for Dad, and he immediately replied, "If you are OK with me pitching in, I'll take care of that."

Kaleigh was not expecting that response but was entirely grateful. "Thank you!" she replied with a hug emoji.

His next text read: "No problem. Have you been to Havenwood?"

She replied, "Not since I picked up his phone and wallet the other day."

"Do you want me to come with you?" Jackson was hoping Kaleigh would reach out for help and was glad to be able to alleviate some of her stress.

"That would be nice. It will be hard to collect his things. I guess I will bring them to my house for now. Wes doesn't seem to want anything to do with any of this. It's so frustrating."

"Today or tomorrow?" Jackson asked.

"Let me call them and see when is a good time," Kaleigh replied. Then she immediately dialed the phone and spoke with the lead nurse. She shared her sorrow and a cute memory of Dad from last week, which brought a smile and a tear to her eye. Kaleigh shared with her the times and places for the Celebration of Life and the luncheon, and they settled on 3:00 p.m. the next day for her to come and pick up Dad's things.

Kaleigh immediately texted Jackson, "Three o'clock tomorrow?"

"Sure, and I can get a suit to the funeral home by tomorrow morning. Will that work for Kelly?" Jackson had waited by his phone for her reply. In fact, he had made sure to turn up his volume as he didn't want to miss any message today from his best friend.

What Kaleigh didn't know was that Jackson had called the nursing home during the pause in messaging and had someone check to see if there was a suit in his dad's closet. Apparently, there were two of them, so he was already planning to go pick one up later. He would leave a message for Kelly that he would be dropping the suit off in the morning. Jackson was grateful not only that Kaleigh had asked him for help but that he was able to do the task.

****

The next afternoon, Kaleigh thought to stop by the lawyer's office. It wasn't that she was checking up on Wesley but that she was trying to avoid an argument. She was driving right by, and it was too early to go to the nursing home anyway. There was another client ahead of her, and the secretary paused her conversation for a moment and asked Kaleigh to please sign in.

Not typically nosy, Kaleigh noticed that she was signing on the last line of the page, and her eyes just happened to rise up toward the top of the paper. She saw her dad's shaky handwriting and the date, which was just over two months ago. A lump came to her throat, and she wasn't sure why. But two months ago, Dad wasn't driving, so someone must have driven him here. Why? These were definite questions she wanted to ask Dan, dad's lawyer. She could not wait for Wesley. Who knew when or if he would follow through with her request to make an appointment with the lawyer? Kaleigh at least needed to know if there was a life insurance policy that could help with costs this week.

Once the person ahead of her was taken care of, she spoke with the secretary and made an appointment for Thursday afternoon, the day after the funeral. She was able to find out that there was a life insurance policy, and that once Kelly sent her the death certificate, she could process that request for her to help with the costs that this week would bring.

Upon walking over to the sign-out sheet to write the sign-out time, Kaleigh thought to quietly snap a picture of her dad's signature and date. Then she texted Kelly and asked her to send a copy of the death certificate to the lawyer's office as soon as possible. The lump in Kaleigh's throat was still there as she walked back to her car.

****

Soon afterward, Kaleigh met Jackson at the entrance to Havenwood. He gave her a hug and asked how she was doing.

"I'm OK" was all she could say. She could not get her father's signature and his visit to the lawyer's office out of her mind, but she wasn't ready to speak the truth into existence yet.

They walked into Havenwood together, Jackson holding each door for her like a true gentleman. The staff had all of Dad's belongings in boxes and crates, five of them in total. They offered a cart on wheels for the two to take the items to the car. Kaleigh had not finished finding homes for many of Mom and Dad's items, which currently lived in her basement. The thought of organizing and finding homes for what was left would be a big task, and she was guessing that Wesley would not want any part of it. That job would be all hers, and it would have to wait until summertime.

Jackson and Kaleigh sat in her car for another ten minutes and talked about Wednesday's events and what still needed to be taken care of. Making the photo board and stopping by the florist to check on the flowers was on her list for the next day. She had decided on a small wake right before the service on Wednesday so as not to draw out the sadness into a second day. Jackson let her know that the suit had been dropped off to Kelly. He also told her he wanted to take her out to dinner tonight but that he had an important delivery to take care of first. They decided that he would pick her up at six o'clock to give him plenty of time to make his delivery and go home to change. They hugged, and Jackson left and walked back to his truck.

CHAPTER 10

After leaving Havenwood, Kaleigh decided to stop at the store on her way home. She needed a few groceries and some shampoo. It wasn't long before she was pulling onto her street, and her heart skipped a beat. A car with a Texas license plate was parked on the street in front of her house.

Thoughts of "Oh my gosh, is it Jeremy!" ran through her head. Over the weekend, Kaleigh had texted him that the Celebration of Life was indeed going to be Wednesday, and he had replied, "OK, no problem! See you soon!" And that was all that was said. The two had been so busy, and Jeremy had decided to just keep his date and time of arrival a surprise.

She parked in the garage and then ran around to the porch, running into his arms for a strong embrace. Jeremy kissed the top of her head like an older brother would do, and then the two hugged once more.

"I can't believe you're here! I mean, I guess I knew you were coming, but I've been so busy I haven't had time to think about it or even to send you a message asking when!" She felt like her voice was rambling with her excitement.

Just then, she grabbed her keys, unlocked the door, turned on the outside lights, and led him into her house.

"I am so glad that I was able to come! I left yesterday morning and got a hotel halfway here. I'm off until Monday, so I can stay the rest of the week." Jeremy shared these plans with her as he picked up his suitcase and bag and followed her inside.

Kaleigh was so excited and happy that her friend was there. She immediately poured them a drink and came into the living room. They began to catch up on all the good and bad that had happened to them since they last saw each other.

At six o'clock on the dot, Jackson pulled his truck into a parking space at the park across the street from Kaleigh's house. It was a gorgeous night, and he felt like walking. As he came closer to her house, just getting ready to cross the street, he noticed a car parked in front of her house. When he looked up, he saw Kaleigh through her front window, sitting next to a guy on her couch, laughing.

At that moment, Jackson's heart sank to what seemed like his ankles. What had happened? Kaleigh didn't mention any company coming over. They did agree that going to dinner tonight was good, didn't they? Who was she talking to? All these thoughts were racing through his head as he stood there, frozen, on the sidewalk. A minute later, he made the decision to go home.

Jeremy and Kaleigh talked for an hour before deciding to order pizza and wings. They were too comfortable and were having such a good conversation that they didn't want to move to a restaurant. As Kaleigh picked up her cell phone to dial the pizza place, she noticed the time and her heart sank. The clock read six-thirty, and she realized that she had completely forgotten about her dinner with Jackson. She had let him down again. Quickly, she sent a text saying, "I'm so sorry" and added, "My friend Jeremy surprised me and drove in from Texas. Can I take a raincheck?"

She felt awful, but there wasn't anything she could do at this moment. There was still no reply. She tried not to let the sadness of her mess-up with Jackson affect her great conversation with Jeremy.

For the rest of the night, all she could do was enjoy her friend's company. They talked until almost ten o'clock, and then Kaleigh showed him to the guest room and adjoining bathroom. She really did like that feature about her house, even though she never really had any company. Their family was just the three of them—Dad, Wesley, and her—since Mom had passed. Dad had a sister, but she had passed away ten years ago. The aunts, uncles, and grandparents had all died years earlier. There was one cousin, a girl named Lola, whom they hadn't seen in years, and last she knew she still lived just one state over. Kaleigh had pretty much lost touch with her, except for an occasional text message, maybe twice per year lately. Their lives were far apart, with seemingly nothing in common. While she was growing up, there wasn't much of a relationship between them as their families never traveled to see each other. There was the occasional family reunion throughout the years, but that was the only time she remembered seeing her cousin. As soon as plans were made at the funeral home, however, she had thought to send Lola a message. Kaleigh had not yet gotten a reply.

There wouldn't be many at the cemetery for the burial, but that was OK with her. Lola would be on the list to come to the cemetery, if she came. The day would be sweet and sad and quiet, just as her father would have wanted it.

****

Kaleigh was grateful she still had eggs in her refrigerator for the morning. They would have to go to the grocery store later, as the rest of her refrigerator was bare, but eggs and coffee would be a good start to the day. It would be later in the afternoon before she was able to tackle the photo board. Kaleigh had kept a box of photographs upstairs that she found when going through her dad's house. She knew that it would be a sad but not impossible task. Jeremy was a huge help. He ran all of the errands with her, carried things for her, and helped her find the best photos for the memory board. Kelly had called and asked if she had anyone in mind for the two readings that were chosen. Jeremy immediately volunteered. Kaleigh was happy that he wanted to step in, as she wasn't sure she could handle speaking in front of people tomorrow.

Something inside her made her mind stop for a second. It's like everything stood still for a moment until Kaleigh heard Kelly on the other line saying, "Hello, are you there?"

Collecting herself, she said, "Oh, yes. Hey, Kelly, can I call you right back?"

"Sure."

And in that moment, she knew what she had to do. She excused herself from Jeremy's company, took her phone, went to the sunroom, and dialed the phone.

Just as she was beginning to think that he would not answer, she heard his voice.

"Hello," Jackson answered.

"Hi." Kaleigh felt as if she was speaking in slow motion. She had not rehearsed what she was going to say. "I am so sorry about last night. I knew Jeremy was coming, but I had no idea when. He's my friend from college. I mean, there's nothing between us, but he is staying for the week. I feel terrible about our dinner plans last night. I will make it up to you." She paused because, at this point, she knew she was rambling and decided it was best to stop talking.

"It's OK. I mean, it threw me for a loop, but I understand." Jackson was trying hard to sound relaxed and not upset, even though the thought of her with Jeremy made his stomach turn.

"OK, good." She paused and then remembered what she wanted to ask him. "Umm, a question for you."

"Yes?" he replied in a curious tone.

"Would you do one of the readings tomorrow at Dad's service? I mean, he has always been fond of you, and I don't think that I will be able to get up in front of people tomorrow." She waited quietly as Jackson processed her request.

"Yes, you know I would do anything for you," Jackson replied in his calm, steady voice.

"Thank you," Kaleigh said as her heart settled a bit. "And again, I owe you dinner."

"Yes, you do." Jackson smiled as he said, "Have a goodnight." He tried not to sound jealous, though he was. He didn't like the fact that someone else was helping his Kaleigh, even though she had said Jeremy was just a friend.

When she got back to the living room, Jeremy had laid out some really amazing photos on the board. Nothing was glued yet, but he had placed some very sweet pictures in what seemed to be perfect places. There was a photo of Dad with his father outside of the Garden Center that Grandpa had started so many years ago. There were childhood pictures of Dad in black and white and sweet pictures of their family of four in color. There was a great mix of photographs throughout the years. Kaleigh didn't know what to say. As she sat down, she found herself gently running her fingers across the photos on the board, stopping at the last picture she had of their family of four. Then her eyes looked up toward the top of the board and saw their family of four when Kaleigh was probably five years old, and another one of just Kaleigh and her dad planting flowers just a couple of years ago. Oh, how she missed those moments.

Jeremy had done a perfect job.

"What do you think?" he said. "I mean, I think I need about three more photos, and you can move things around."

"No, don't move a thing. It's . . . it's perfect." Kaleigh interrupted him as a tear ran down her cheek. "Don't move a thing, I love it." She repeated." And she laid her head back on the couch, closed her eyes, took some deep breaths, and rested.

CHAPTER 11

The day of the funeral had arrived. Kaleigh had mixed emotions. Neither emotion was happy, but rather a mixture of sadness as she thought of all her dad had meant to her, and relief that she hoped would come when this day was over. She also felt some worry about telling Wesley that she had made an appointment with the lawyer for tomorrow. She had to tell him but didn't know how he would react. These thoughts ran through her head as she headed to the kitchen and made coffee and toast for breakfast.

Then a thought came into her mind. *If Wesley had called the lawyer's office, the secretary would have told him that an appointment had already been made. He would have then texted her—unhappy, but at least she would have heard from him.* There had been no such text, so this must mean that he hadn't called the office yet. Still, she had to tell him today.

Jeremy and Kaleigh walked into the funeral home together. Jackson was there and saw the two walk in. He noticed Jeremy putting his hand on Kaleigh's shoulder as she shook hands with Kelly's right-hand man, the co-manager of the funeral home. Jackson told himself everything would be fine today, that he had no reason to be jealous, but when he saw Jeremy, his heart sank again.

A moment later, Kaleigh walked over to Jackson and gave him a hug. Then she introduced Jeremy, and the two shook hands. Kelly pulled Kaleigh away to take care of some last-minute questions, and the two men were left alone. It was awkward at first, but the two were able to have a good conversation about college, their favorite sports teams, and briefly, their shared friendship with Kaleigh.

Jackson had never officially met Jeremy before that day, but he seemed like a nice guy. Kaleigh had said there were no romantic feelings between them, but that didn't mean he wasn't jealous. Jackson should have been the one walking in with her, helping her through this difficult day, but he soon realized that wouldn't be the case.

Kaleigh had set her shawl and purse on two chairs in the front row, one for her and one for Jeremy. Her mind was so full she wasn't thinking of saving a seat for Jackson. It was Jeremy who walked up with her to the casket, hand on her back, supporting her. All Jackson could do was sit back and watch. He didn't like the knot that sat in his stomach.

Kelly came up to Jackson and gave him a copy of the service with his reading circled. Immediately he noticed he was the second reading, not sure who would be reading the first.

Wesley walked in toward the end of the calling hour. He gave Kaleigh a quick hug and stepped back. He seemed uncomfortable and kept shifting his weight as he spoke with Kaleigh, Jeremy, and others who came by to pay their respects.

The service was short and sweet, and the knot in Jackson's stomach grew when he realized it was Jeremy who was doing the first reading. When Jackson came to the microphone, he struggled to keep his voice steady and calm. He was sad for Kaleigh, as he knew how much her father had meant to her. He was jealous of Jeremy, as he was the one who got to be close to her on this day. It should have been him by her side, not the guy from Texas. But he took a deep breath and spoke, pushing the thoughts of jealousy to the side. This day was not supposed to be about him, and he was beginning to realize that maybe he needed to get over her. That was all there was to it. Simple, just get over Kaleigh. Yeah, right.

As things wrapped up at the funeral home and most of the guests had gone outside, Jackson overheard Jeremy say, "Are you ready, Leigh?" as he put her shawl around her shoulders.

"Yes," she replied as he grabbed her hand, and the two walked out the front door. Jackson had never heard anyone but her father call her by that name. *How did . . .when did Jeremy get to call her Leigh?*

His jealousy was starting to get the better of him. He tried to shake it off as he walked out the door.

Jackson was lucky enough to grab a seat on the other side of Kaleigh at the luncheon. It did not feel right to sit at another table. Even though he had realized this morning that he probably needed to move on, he still was drawn to her and wanted to support her. It was a tug-of-war at this moment with his heart, but he did his best to stay cool and be friendly to everyone, even Jeremy. Wesley sat across from them, and the four were able to have a nice conversation as they were served lunch. There were probably forty people there—a nice mix of neighbors, friends, and employees. The invites to the cemetery were few, and the small group would leave in an hour and a half to bring Dad to his final resting place.

Wesley was the first to get up from the lunch table, even though not everyone had finished eating. It was then that Kaleigh quickly excused herself from the table, telling Jeremy and Jackson that she would be right back.

As she caught up to Wesley, she said, "Hey, I need to tell you something before we go to the cemetery." "What?" he said as he turned around.

"I . . . I made an appointment for tomorrow at the lawyer's office." She had hesitated as she was dreading his response.

"Oh, OK," Wesley's reply startled her. This was not what she was expecting. She paused in astonishment but then realized it was her turn to talk.

"Can you meet me tomorrow at two p.m.?" Kaleigh asked.

"I don't know. Can you remind me tomorrow, and I will check? It will depend on staffing." Wesley again looked uncomfortable in his skin as he shifted his weight from one foot to the other. He looked at her another moment, looked away, and said, "I'm going to head to the cemetery." He looked back at Kaleigh once more, then walked out the door. Jackson followed Jeremy and Kaleigh to the cemetery. Three of Dad's closest friends from the Garden Center came, along with Kelly, Danielle and her husband Chris. They had missed the service and luncheon, but school was over by now and they were able to make it to this part of the day. Kaleigh was happy to see her and they hugged for a good minute at least.

They each set a rose on Dad's casket before the prayers. Afterward, each person took two stones, one to throw under the casket to send a wish or say a prayer, and one to keep to remember dad. The prayer service was short, but it felt like the closure Kaleigh needed after these last few crazy years. It was a beautiful way to say goodbye.

As everyone slowly walked toward their cars, Kaleigh stopped Wesley, saying, "Hey, do you want to come over for a drink?" She felt like she should extend an olive branch to her brother. She really did feel bad that all of the family business now rested on his shoulders. Kaleigh didn't want to lose her brother, her only family.

"No, I really gotta get back to work," He said as he turned and finished walking to his car.

"OK," she called out, "You know where I live if you change your mind." But Wesley continued to walk away.

As Jackson began to walk to his car, Kaleigh caught up with him. "You are welcome to come over for a drink." She said as she gently put her hand on his arm.

"Thanks for the offer but I really need to get back to work." He lied but thought it made for a good excuse. As much as he thought Jeremy seemed like a nice guy, he still felt awkward about being in Kaleigh's house when he was there.

Jackson gave Kaleigh one more hug and told her to call him if she needed anything. Then he shook hands with Jeremy and left. It was a habit of his to tell Kaleigh to call him. However, it was then that he realized that he should probably work to break the habit of asking her to call him.

Danielle and Chris came over and the four talked for over an hour. It was nice to laugh again, to relax with friends, to have the work and dread of planning this day behind her. Kaleigh, in her heart, was hoping that Wesley or Jackson would change their mind, come to the door. She tried not to let this get to her, as the company she did have was truly great.

****

The next morning, Jeremy offered to take her out to breakfast. The two could talk forever, and they ended up sitting for nearly three hours as they ate and had their coffee refilled again and again. The diner really did have the best cup of coffee in town. She was never sure what they added to it, but it was smooth, sweet, and delicious.

Once they talked about their futures and what things looked like, Jeremy turned the conversation to Jackson. He mentioned to Kaleigh that he noticed Jackson squirming a little yesterday, and he felt that, at times, that he was in the way. During yesterday's events, it seemed difficult for Jeremy to know where to stand and if he should take a break and give Jackson a turn. Jeremy had felt that there might be something between the two. There was one point at the luncheon when Kaleigh and Jackson were laughing, and she rested her head on his shoulder for a moment, wiping a tear that had fallen during their laughter. Jeremy did not mention this during their conversation, but it had come to his mind. He wanted happiness and love for his best friend. He knew *they* weren't meant to be, but he wanted that for Kaleigh, that deep passionate love with *her* person.

The funny thing was, Jeremy wasn't jealous at all. Even after all the time they had shared together during college, the crashing at each other's places, and the shared sadness of the deaths of their mothers, there wasn't ever any spark of love. Sure, there was a deep friendship there, one of understanding, deep caring, and respect, but it never seemed to blossom into anything else, and he was OK with that.

Kaleigh listened intently to her friend, then paused as she didn't know where to begin the story. She hadn't shared much about Jackson in all of their conversations through the years. After another moment he decided to start the story back to when Dad had taken the fall, and she and Wesley had decided to give fresh produce sales a try. She spoke of their trips to Rita's or to the coffee shop just to talk. Then she told him how out-of-the-loop she was on the day of their friends' wedding when Jackson sprung his feelings upon her. She mentioned feeling dumb and how she felt as if she was at a loss for words. She also expressed how awful she felt for turning him down. Kaleigh added that, in looking back, she thought it was probably for the better, as she wasn't in love with him at the time. At this point she took another sip of coffee and placed her hands around the cup, letting the next thought come into her mind. "Lately, I am beginning to think that, I might be feeling more." She shared all of this with Jeremy, and he listened intently.

Jeremy knew his friend and wanted to give her time and space to think. Kaleigh had told him about her nightmares, confiding in him one night during a horrible storm last year. When Kaleigh shared the night Jackson was there during one of her bad dreams, she felt chills thinking about how truly amazing Jackson was to take such great care of her. As Kaleigh was sharing these memories with Jeremy, she began to realize even more that maybe she was developing feelings for Jackson. It was as if her heart and her mind were waking up out of a clouded dream and coming into reality. In that one moment her heart seemed to skip a beat and she blushed as she smiled. Then the next moment, she found herself speaking her inner-most thoughts, "Oh gosh, what if I've messed this up? I have to talk to him."

At that same moment, Jeremy spoke the same words, "I think you should talk to him." Jeremy had read her mind.

"Yeah, I really need to," she answered back as she took another sip of coffee.

"Love doesn't always happen overnight, you know? Take my sister Julia. She and Jacob were friends for a long time before they realized there was more to it. It doesn't happen in a snap for everyone."

Jeremy had a point, a very good point.

When they were leaving breakfast, Kaleigh asked Jeremy if he minded if she made a phone call. He told her that he didn't mind at all and decided to go ahead of her to the car to check his email. It had been a while since he had checked it, and he figured it would only make life easier when he got home if he cleaned out some of it here.

Kaleigh walked down the sidewalk, took a deep breath, and dialed the phone. "Hello," Jackson answered.

"Hey, stranger. How are you?" Kaleigh tried to keep her voice light, though she was nervous and her heart was racing.

"I'm OK," he replied and then got quiet.

"Hey, do you want to grab dinner on Saturday? I'd love to catch up with you."

After that, there was silence. Jackson didn't know what to say. He had come to the realization that he needed some space so that if he took a break, maybe he could begin the process of letting her go. Upon realizing he had left the conversation in an awkward pause, he knew in that moment that he needed to say something.

"Umm, my sister invited me to go to dinner with her that night. Can I take a raincheck?" That was all he could think of. It was a lie, of course, but seemed like a good excuse, nonetheless.

"Oh, OK, just let me know when you're free." Kaleigh was shocked at his response but tried hard to keep her voice lighthearted and not shaky. No one said anything for a few moments, so they both just said goodbye. When Kaleigh hung up the phone she took a moment to catch her breath and thought about how his voice sounded different. He had never given her an answer like that before. It sounded almost not caring, like a brush-off. That wasn't like Jackson at all.

Maybe he truly was busy. She hoped he would reach out and ask her to go out soon. Her thoughts trailed off as she noticed Jeremy sitting in her car, typing on his phone. She was disappointed but realized she should get back to her friend and slowly began to walk toward her car.

As she sat down in the driver's seat, she immediately thought about her brother and the fact that she forgot to remind him of their appointment with the lawyer that day. She sent him a quick message before she and Jeremy took a drive.

They drove past the first house Kaleigh's parents had owned, the one where both she and Wesley came home from the hospital. It was cute—small but cute. Then they drove past the house where Kaleigh had the most memories. This was the only other house they had lived in growing up—the one where they celebrated birthdays, graduations, afternoons of baking wonderful treats, and evenings working in the garden. It was also the one that Mom never came home to that terrible night, and the one Dad could no longer live in. Kaleigh had worked with a realtor just two years ago to sell the cute house. The emotions were mixed, but Kaleigh realized that she needed to say goodbye to the house one more time to help close this chapter in her life. Jeremy looked over at her, saw a tear running down her cheek, and took her hand as if to say, I understand, and I'm here for you.

Chapter 12

Jeremy and Kaleigh drove over to the lawyer's office for the afternoon appointment. Before getting out of the car, Kaleigh thought to check her phone. A text had come in from her brother: "Sorry, can't make it today."

After letting out a sigh, Kaleigh quietly said, "I knew he wouldn't come. Why am I surprised?"

"Wes isn't coming?" Jeremy clarified.

"No, he's not," Kaleigh said and felt a big let-down. Why was she surprised, though? It wasn't like he had helped with anything else this week. For a moment she thought how she was actually surprised he showed up to the funeral. As that thought came into her head, she told herself, "Well that's not fair, of course he would come to that." After one more sigh, she grabbed her purse and exited the car.

"Want me to come?" Jeremy got out of the car too, and figured if she said no then he would take a walk.

"Sure, I could use the company," she replied, and he held the door open for her as they walked inside.

Dan was hesitant to share the exact information from the estate without Wesley present, so he kept the conversation to the life insurance policy. There was enough to cover the cost of yesterday, all of the events, the flowers, and even the luncheon at the Tavern. There was also some left to take care of the outstanding balance from Havenwood, and after all of that was paid, she and Wesley would split the rest. It was never about the money for Kaleigh. She just wanted all of this behind her and Dad's wishes granted. Dan had received the certificate from Kelly and said he would take care of everything. Kaleigh thanked him for making everything so easy. Kaleigh couldn't bring herself to ask about dad's signature on the sign-in sheet. The voice inside her head was nagging her but she just couldn't do it.

On her way out, she thought to ask Dan if Wesley had contacted him to set up a time to read the will. His answer was "No, not yet." She started walking away, then at the last minute asked if he had time next Thursday evening. She figured near closing time at the Garden Center might be better and less busy, making it easier for Wesley to come. She felt like maybe Wesley would never call, and she just wanted the I's dotted and the T's crossed so that everything was done and behind her. She was ready to move on with her life.

Dan checked with his secretary and put their meeting on the calendar for six o'clock next Thursday evening. Kaleigh put the date and time in her phone, then sent it to Wesley. She wasn't expecting a response but needed to let him know.

As Jeremy drove her home she seemed quiet. The thought of "Why wouldn't he come?" ran through her mind. Her thoughts then moved to "Is Wesley that hardened that he couldn't come and listen to the lawyer?" and "Why hasn't he called to make an appointment? Wesley, for sure, had a vested interest in the future of the store and in Dad's assets." Then her thoughts turned to the store. "Maybe I should call Teddy to see what help they need at the store. Maybe I just need to talk to Wes some more." Kaleigh wasn't sure if she wanted to go back to working at the Garden Center, but that didn't mean that she couldn't help make a plan that would give Wesley a break, some help, and some peace of mind. She did not hate her brother. She was just frustrated. As the older sister, she felt like she needed to step in and help in some way.

"You OK?" Jeremy asked after about five minutes of quiet as he drove.

"Yeah, I just have a lot running through my head, mostly about Wes."

"What's going on with him?" Jeremy asked, not knowing if she would have any real information to share.

Kaleigh took a deep breath and told him the story of last week at Dan's office—the sign-in sheet, the shaky signature, and even the fact that she took a photo of it. She shared her feelings and thoughts, reflecting on the fact that two months ago, Dad's memory was gone. That he could not have made any decisions and would be unable to even come up with questions to ask the lawyer let alone drive there.

All Jeremy could do was listen. He didn't know what to think, but when he combined what he noticed about Wesley's behavior yesterday with the story, it started to appear as if Wesley was guilty of something. Jeremy thought about sharing these thoughts with Kaleigh but then decided against it. All of this was too fresh, too recent, and he only had a small amount of evidence to go on. Instead, he decided to keep these thoughts for another time.

"What are you going to do?" Jeremy asked in his caring voice as he pressed on the break, approaching the stop sign.

"I don't know." Kaleigh quietly replied as she let out a sigh.

Jeremy stayed quiet, to let Kaleigh think, then pointed straight and then left, asking which way they should go.

"Oh, straight, let's stop at the store. I don't have much to cook for dinner. I kind of feel like being home tonight, if you don't mind." Kaleigh was speaking in a quiet, slower voice as her head felt heavy with all the questions spinning around in it.

"Sure thing," replied Jeremy, and he slowly pressed his foot on the gas.

That night, Jeremy tried his best to cheer her up as he turned the conversation to memories from college. They laughed as they cooked together. Jeremy had offered to make his famous (he claimed based upon his family's reaction), chicken parmesan if Kaleigh took care of the pasta and salad. She had fun cooking with someone else, talking, laughing, and just enjoying the company. Jeremy helped her forget about her worries for a while, and the evening was nice. After cleaning up dinner, Kaleigh realized how tired she was and asked Jeremy if he minded if she went to bed.

"Not at all," he replied in his understanding way. "Any ideas of what you want to do tomorrow?"

"Something fun," she replied.

"OK, something fun it is! Goodnight, my friend."

"Goodnight, my friend!" she replied.

****

The next day was wonderful. The two had decided to pack a cooler with drinks and snacks, fill up the gas tank, and just take a drive—no plans, no rules, just seeing where the day would take them. It was so nice and it let Kaleigh let go of reality for a bit. She was able to block the worries and the sadness out of her head for a few hours and just enjoy the company of a great friend.

They ended up at the beach, strolling along the boardwalk. Then they went into a small museum of wax figures that was truly amazing and had ice cream sundaes for lunch as if they were kids sharing an awesome birthday treat. Growing up they each had memories of, on a few occasions, their parents each letting them have ice cream for a meal, and how they thought that was the greatest. This brought back sweet thoughts and was a fun trip down memory lane.

The only serious thing they discussed was which subject Kaleigh should focus on for her master's degree. Now that she had more free time, she felt like this was the perfect next step. The school district would help her pay for it. All she had to do was complete the paperwork, make the first payment, and choose her preferred major.

The rest of the day was spent reminiscing about their college days, talking of Jeremy and whether he had anyone special in his life. They found themselves playing "Have You Ever" like they did in college. Jeremy didn't come out and say that he was in love. However, he did talk about a woman named Jenny, whom he was speaking with online. He had never pictured himself using a dating app, but a friend of his at work had had luck and dared Jeremy to try it. He was being cautious and taking things slow, but they seemed to have a lot in common and had just begun talking on the phone. He shared how much she makes him laugh and how talking with her for two hours seems like only minutes. Kaleigh was happy for him. Jeremy was such an amazing guy and any girl would be lucky to have him.

Kaleigh and Jeremy ended up at a small miniature golf place on the side of the road as they explored the area. Kaleigh surprised herself with a steady hand and a lower score than Jeremy. Jeremy was not on his A game that day and had many golf balls that went off-course. The two laughed as his second ball tumbled into the water and he had to ask the clerk for yet another golf ball so he could continue to play. The look the clerk gave him as he asked for yet another golf ball, as if Jeremy was a five year old kid who had been messing around all afternoon, was priceless. The two couldn't stop laughing and would hold onto that memory forever.

It had been a long time since Kaleigh let go of responsibilities and just went shopping. Jeremy was sweet and let her go into four or five stores, browsing for anything that caught her eye. There was a beach-themed store with coasters, pictures, dishes, and knick-knacks. Then a jewelry store, where Kaleigh found a beautiful silver necklace, and a couple of clothing stores, one more fancy and one casual. Kaleigh found some cute clothes at both stores, some for work and some for around town. She couldn't resist adding in a couple of pairs of shoes. It had been so long since she had bought new clothes for herself. Jeremy was very patient and didn't seem annoyed at all.

On their way out of the beach town, they found an Italian restaurant for dinner before making the drive back home. The conversation shifted from fun to more serious, and they each shared ideas of what they should do the next time they got together. They made a pact that they would not let so many years pass by before they got together again.

Kaleigh thanked Jeremy immensely for this much-needed day away from home. She would remember this special day forever. As they drove, Kaleigh thought, *My heart is sad, my path is still unclear, will I find clarity? Will there be a sign of what I should do next?* She hoped for clarity more than anything now. She wanted to know what her path should be in her education, in life, and in love. Was there true love in her future? Would Jackson come back to her, or had she lost him even as a friend? Was it he that she was meant to be with or someone else? Either way, she could not imagine walking through the rest of her life alone.

Chapter 13

After Jeremy left that Saturday morning, she threw a load of laundry in and then found herself on the couch with a cup of coffee. Yesterday's drive to the beach, being able to let go of reality for a bit, was amazing. She would not have traded the time with Jeremy for anything. They were memories that she would never forget, but it felt good to be home in her quiet house on this cloudy Saturday.

There was so much to think about, so many questions, and so many unknowns. She hadn't heard from Jackson, although this was the day he was supposed to go to dinner with his sister. And she needed to talk to Wesley. She hadn't heard anything from him since the funeral. He hadn't answered her text yet about the meeting with Dan next week. The thought came into Kaleigh's mind that maybe he needed space. Everyone grieves in their own way, so maybe Wesley just needed time. She decided not to bother him this weekend. She decided to give him space.

She could call Danielle, as it was the weekend. Danielle would drop everything for her if she asked. No, Kaleigh decided. She shouldn't bother Danielle, and it turned out she wasn't actually in the mood for company. That was when her eyes went to the bookshelf next to the fireplace. She saw her father's box of photos, and next to it was the scrapbook her mother had given her on the last birthday she spent with her mother. Suddenly, she found herself turning its pages, taking a trip down memory lane.

It wasn't long before the memories came flooding back: days when her mom would dance with her in their kitchen and afternoons when she and her mom would bake together. The two of them would often bring cookies to Havenwood at holiday time, bringing smiles to the residents there. Kaleigh would watch in awe at how her mom made everyone around her smile.

Kaleigh's mom had been a teacher, and upon retiring, had turned into a chef in the kitchen. She would cook for families who were going through tough times or just to spoil a neighbor. At least once a month she would bring treats to the nursing home, and Kaleigh would tag along. There was a picture of the two of them at Christmas time, standing near Santa Claus at the Havenwood Christmas party. She must have been around seven years old. Wesley didn't often come to Havenwood, but would choose to go with their dad to the Garden Center instead.

Kaleigh knew that she got her teacher spirit from her mom but wasn't sure whether her mom had also given her the gift of cooking. Maybe when all of this was over, she would try her hand in the kitchen. She just hadn't had the time to focus on cooking or baking. Since graduating college, there was always something keeping her too busy to have much time to cook. The pictures in the scrapbook of her spending time with her mother in the kitchen all those years ago brought a sweet smile to her face.

And then there was her dad. Turning the page, she saw a picture of the two of them in the fields, digging in the dirt. Kaleigh's face was so happy. She figured she must have been about eight, with her lavender shovel, matching boots, and hat. She had always loved that color. Her dad had dirt on his face and a baseball cap on his head, and they both looked up at the camera with big smiles! Growing up, Kaleigh was happy, both cooking in the kitchen with her mom and digging in the dirt with her dad.

As it turned out, Kaleigh did end up with a green thumb and knew that she got that gift from her dad. When she had bought her house, her dad let her pick out all the shrubs, trees, and flowers she wanted, and they worked together to fix up the landscaping. Every year, her neighbors commented on how beautiful her yard was. She knew exactly what each plant needed and kept a beautiful garden bed next to and around her sidewalk. She was grateful for all her father had taught her throughout the years. Gardening came easily to her, and she loved taking care of her little plants.

Kaleigh really was lucky to have such amazing parents growing up. She truly did miss them. They had done so much for her, and she loved them and missed them dearly. She wished she had had more time with them but felt grateful for what a wonderful childhood she had. Her parents were so very much in love. As she turned the page again, her eyes immediately went to a photo of them sharing a seat in an Adirondack chair, Mom sitting next to Dad, her arms around him, both laughing. Even in their older years, she had seen them be affectionate with each other, holding hands while walking by the river on a Sunday afternoon. She remembered them leaving sweet notes with a rubber band on the coffee creamer in the refrigerator. Both drank coffee each morning, Dad in a travel mug on his way to the store, Mom on her way to school. She guessed they had thought it was the perfect place so that in the rush of the morning, the notes wouldn't be missed.

Kaleigh remembered her mom telling her that she had met Dad in high school but they both had gone to prom with someone else. The story was that, after graduation, both of their prom dates had decided to cut ties as they were leaving for college and wanted a fresh start. While going to the community college, Kaleigh's mom worked at the bakery and made good money there. Dad often stopped by on his lunch break for fresh coffee. The friendship and the feelings grew, and before they knew it, the two had a standing date each Friday night at the local Italian restaurant. Two years later, they were married, and the rest was history. She became a teacher, he took over the Garden Center for his father, and they bought the little house on Danbury Lane.

To Kaleigh, it seemed like her mom's path just kind of fell into place. The two were so happy, and the relationship just seemed to happen naturally. From what she heard, their friendship turned into love very quickly, and they both just knew. Their paths crossed, came together and everything fell into place for them.

Kaleigh took a deep breath as she closed the scrapbook. What about her? Why had her path to love, even her path to finding happiness, been so difficult? She was lucky to have such great friends in Jeremy and Jackson and now Danielle. And she was grateful for everything her three friends had done for her. Before this moment, she hadn't really had time to think about herself—what she wanted and what she needed. But now that her parents were gone and having no idea where her relationship with Wesley stood, and for that matter, Jackson, suddenly she felt empty. It was like she was standing alone in the dark, needing and wanting someone to walk with her. The first person that came to her mind was Jackson. She found herself missing him, wondering what he was doing. Was her path leading toward him or away? Would her path ever lead her to true happiness, like the happiness and love that her parents had?

As these thoughts rushed through her head, her eyes were drawn to a double photo frame sitting on her bookshelf. Each picture was of her parents on the front steps of the last house they lived in. The two were smiling and happy, Dad holding his baseball cap in one hand and his other arm around Mom's waist. Mom most likely made him take the hat off for the picture. In the next picture, they were on that same porch on the same day, but Dad had leaned in to give Mom a kiss on the cheek.

Kaleigh wanted that. She wondered if her path would take her there—to happiness with a partner who cared for her, who loved her, one who never left her side. She wanted true love, a person who would walk with her through the times of darkness and the times of light. More than ever, Kaleigh wanted that, deeply.

At that moment, she picked up her phone and stared at Jackson's name.

"I hope you have a good dinner tonight with your sis. Call me tomorrow," she texted and hit Send.

****

The next day, by one o'clock, she still hadn't heard from Jackson. This wasn't like him at all. She decided to text him again, "Hey, are you up for coffee today?"

Two hours later, with still no reply from Jackson, she decided to pay him a visit. This was her last day off before heading back to work. She had spent two hours on her computer, getting organized for the week ahead. With no return text from Jackson it was causing her to have a pit in her stomach. The unknown, the silence from him, was making it difficult for her to push past all the sadness.

Kaleigh pulled up to Jackson's house and knocked on the door. There was no answer. His truck was there, so she decided to walk around to see if she could find him. Walking around his apple trees, she heard his voice. He was talking to one of his workers.

"Hey, Jackson!" Kaleigh waved as he came around the corner.

He was surprised to see her, and his heart skipped a beat. As much as he tried to get her out of his mind, he hadn't been able to, and now, as she stood there, with the breeze in her long hair, he realized that letting her go would be the hardest thing he had ever had to do. She looked beautiful, but he had to focus. He had to stay tough so he could work to let her go.

"Hi," he said as he walked past her to get to his truck.

Kaleigh, thinking that was odd, replied, "Want to grab a cup of coffee? I've missed you."

It still hurt that she had forgotten him that night, the night he was going to take her out to dinner. He was beginning to feel like she wanted his company only when it was convenient for her, and his jealousy was still raw.

"I . . . I can't today. I'm just swamped." His tone was rushed and tense.

"Oh, OK. Can you text me later this week, and we can meet up?" She tried to keep her voice light and calm, but inside, her heart was crumbling. What had happened to her friend? Why had he changed? "Yeah" was all he said in reply.

Slowly she walked to her car and sat in the driver's seat, taking a few deep breaths before starting the car. What had she done? Had she really lost her friend, her best friend? Was that what he was, and was that friendship coming to an end?

That night, she called Danielle and told her everything.

"Oh gosh," she began after listening to Kaleigh speak for five minutes, going over everything from the past week. Danielle took a breath before speaking. "Do you think he is jealous of Jeremy?" she began, and Kaleigh realized that she had not even thought about that. So many thoughts immediately began running through her head: "Had she spent too much time with Jeremy? Hadn't she made it clear that Jeremy was just a friend and nothing more? Did Jackson not believe her?"

After she went through all of those questions in her head, she spoke them aloud. "Oh, no, you don't really think he thinks that, do you? I mean, I told him that Jeremy was just a friend from college, that there was nothing romantic between us." Kaleigh was trying to keep from speaking too fast, as her heart and her head were spinning now. "That night that Jeremy came into town and I forgot about dinner . . ." she paused for a moment, ". . . he must be so upset about that. I am such a terrible friend." Kaleigh's heart suddenly hurt as she rubbed her now aching head.

"Well, you know jealousy comes to a person's heart no matter what the story really is." Her friend had a good point. "The mind can twist and turn the truth and make us go to places with our heart, make us think things that aren't true, cause us to ruin what could be beautiful." Danielle's words were wise and true.

All Kaleigh could do was close her eyes and take in those words, those truths about what jealousy can do to people, and agree. "Wow, that was profound. True and profound. When did you get so wise about all of this?"

"Haha," her friend laughed at the other end of the line. "Well, let's just say, in college, I went through severe jealousy with a friend of mine, and it turned my head and my heart upside down." She paused for a moment, then continued, "It caused me to lose a good friend and a boyfriend. It took hold of me and wouldn't let go, wouldn't let me think clearly. I was a mess. I really thought my best friend was stealing my boyfriend, and later I found out none of what I thought was true, but boy did jealousy cause me to make a mess of things. It made me crazy, and pulled my head and my heart in all the wrong directions."

"Wow, I had no idea you had been through all of that." Kaleigh was so appreciative that she had a friend who understood her.

"Yeah, I don't ever talk about it. I mean, it never really comes up in everyday conversation! But, in looking back, it brought me on a different path than I may have gone on if I hadn't made a mess of those relationships at college. It caused me to grow up a lot. When things fell apart I decided to move back home and that's when I found my Chris. You know, looking back on things, that week right before everything blew up in my face at school was like my fork in the road. That next week, the worst of my life, pushed me to take the road to the right, and I am happy with the outcome. I have made peace with everything that happened, and I know that what happened was meant to be."

After a brief moment of silence, Kaleigh asked, "What do I do?"

Sighing, wanting to give her friend the best advice, Danielle answered, "Just give it some time. Maybe space and time is what he needs."

"And what if that doesn't work?" Kaleigh wondered this with her whole heart.

"Well, a big apology. Maybe you write him a letter in a few weeks, tell him everything, when his heart isn't so raw." Danielle had the best advice, she thought. That was just what she would do.

"Thank you, friend. I really needed this." Kaleigh didn't know what she would do without Danielle.

Kaleigh felt defeated and sad but decided to give Jackson his space, if that was what he wanted.

CHAPTER 14

Kaleigh's first week back at school was tough, trying to find her new normal and catch up on all of the work she had missed. She found herself staying late at work just to try to get herself and her classroom reorganized.

By Wednesday afternoon, she was a bit more caught up and decided to stop at the new sandwich shop for a bite to eat on her way home. Sitting by herself next to the window while she waited for her order, she found herself scrolling through pictures on her phone. She was not a huge photographer but did have a few photos of her dad and her in the flower fields, and one of her dad's favorite plants that had grown so beautifully the last year he was at the Garden Center. Then she found a photo of her cousin Lola and her husband. They had gotten married last year, eloped, and she had sent her a photo of the two of them. Anytime someone sent her a photo, which wasn't often, she saved it to her phone. Realizing that she had not heard from Lola yet since her father's passing, Kaleigh decided to reach out again with a text message. She thought for sure she would have heard from Lola by now.

About thirty minutes had passed, and Kaleigh was just finishing her sandwich when a text came through. It was from Lola. "Hi, Kaleigh. Sorry I missed the funeral. I'm so sorry about your dad."

Kaleigh stared at the screen for a moment before replying. "Thank you. How are you doing?"

Kaleigh was not expecting such a quick response, but she had gotten one. "I've been better. Life is kind of upside-down for me right now, which is why I couldn't make it to the funeral. I really wanted to be there."

Wow, this is the most conversation she had had with Lola in years. Kaleigh thought and continued with her reply.

"I'm sorry to hear that. Anything I can do to help?"

For a few minutes, there was no reply. Kaleigh finished her drink, cleared the table, and headed for her car.

No more messages came through from Lola that night. When Kaleigh got home, she remembered to text Wesley again and remind him of the appointment with the lawyer tomorrow night. And again, no response.

Still receiving no response from Lola, she decided to offer help once more. She didn't want her to think she wasn't available to talk or to help. You know, sometimes people offer help but don't really mean it. She did not want to seem like that at all.

She sent one more text: "I'm here for you, cousin. I don't know what you are going through, but if you need anything, please don't hesitate to ask. Love you."

****

After school on Thursday, when she still hadn't heard from Wesley, she decided to go to the Garden Center. When she got there, Wesley was talking to a customer at the front registers. She came up near him so that he would see she was there, but not too close as to be intrusive into the conversation.

Ms. Henney waved to her as she finished paying for her plants, and Tonya came up behind her and gave her a hug. Tonya was in college now but had worked at the store forever. It was good to see her.

When Wesley finished his conversation with the customer, Kaleigh lightly grabbed his arm and said, "Hey, can we talk?" Not sure of his reaction, she tried to keep her touch and her voice playful and calm. "In the office." she added.

"Yeah, I guess," he replied in a surprised tone.

Kaleigh followed him to the office, listening to him give directions to two staff members along the way. He did have a good handle on this place. He was good at what he did. He was organized, polite, and well-liked by the staff. These qualities were important in keeping the store in a good place.

When they entered the office, Wesley headed directly for the desk, put his clipboard down, turned around, leaned up against the desk, and crossed his arms across his chest. "What's up?" he asked.

Her heart began to race a bit out of nervousness, and she took a deep breath before she spoke. "I haven't heard from you," she began. "Everything OK?"

"Yeah, I guess" was all he could say.

"I texted you about meeting the Dan tonight to look at the will, and I hadn't heard back from you." Kaleigh was trying to keep her voice calm. It seemed like she was doing this a lot lately.

"Umm, yeah, I'm sorry, just been busy." He brushed a hand through his hair as he often did when he was nervous.

"Wesley, I miss us, the way we used to talk, tell each other what is going on. We haven't had that in a while. I know you have had a lot to do around here, and I want to help you again if I can. Do you need help with anything?" She wasn't sure what else to say.

"I'm doing OK. I mean, I haven't really thought about you coming back. You've been gone for so long," he said, his voice turning slightly mean.

"Can we figure out how to talk about what happened, what is bothering us, so I can have my brother back?" Kaleigh didn't know how else to say it. She didn't sugar-coat it, just got right to the point.

"Maybe . . . it's just a busy time." He answered rather quickly.

"It's always a busy time, Wes. I want to help you. I want to figure out how the two of us can get back to what we had, a relationship where we talk, actually talk, once a week."

Wesley was silent as he ran his fingers through his hair.

At least Kaleigh had said what she needed to. She paused for a moment longer and then asked, "Are you coming to Dan's office at six o'clock?" and was hoping he would say yes.

"I'm going to try. I know I should be there. Tony did say he could close." He paused another moment, picked up his clipboard and said, "I'll try." And with that, he walked away.

****

Kaleigh didn't know why she was nervous, but she was, as she walked into the lawyer's office at five minutes to six. She signed in again and waited in the lobby. The office was very quiet as she was sure the secretary had left for the day.

Dan came out of the office and Kaleigh stood up to shake his hand.

"Is Wes joining us in person or on the phone?" Dan asked.

Kaleigh hadn't thought of that option. "I don't know, I can call him." She grabbed her phone out of her purse.

Surprisingly, after just one ring, Wesley answered, "I'm on my way. Give me three minutes."

When Wesley walked in, he looked nervous and rushed. He had a seat, not next to her but across from her, in Dan's office.

"OK, let's get to it," Dan spoke quickly. "You both know that your dad was a pretty simple man. I mean, he didn't need or want any bells or whistles, so you will see that his will reflects that."

Both Wesley and Kaleigh remained quiet.

"As you know, you are the only close living relatives left in the family, so everything left in his estate is gifted to only the two of you. That makes things pretty easy. And there is no house, just the account with the cash from the house sale a couple of years ago and then the business."

Kaleigh's heart was fluttering a little, and there was no reason for her to be nervous. It was just a final step to splitting up Dad's assets, no big deal.

Dan continued, "So, the cash that is left from the sale of the house gets split fifty-fifty. I have papers drawn up for you both to sign advising the bank to give you each a check for half of what is left in the account, and then you can do with that what you wish. The contents of the house were already sold and taken care of previously, I am guessing, so nothing about that is in the will. Whatever is left there, you two can work that out."

"Any money from the sale of the furniture and other items from Dad's house I had deposited in his account, so that is included already." Kaleigh added, wanting to clarify that piece of information.

"Perfect." Dan replied.

"Now, for the business," Dan moved his glasses down on his nose a touch, ready to read from a piece of paper. After reading the current value of the business, including the land it sits on and the fields surrounding it, Dan paused and said, "This will be split, eighty percent to Wesley, twenty percent to Kaleigh." At this point Dan looked up, pushed his glasses up and continued, "Now should one of you want to buy the other out of the business, I can always help you with that. That is always an option. If you want to keep things the same, all we have to do is sign some papers to make the new ownership of the business official. Your dad didn't want any fuss or to make anything difficult. You know he just wanted you both to be happy."

After a moment, Dan asked, "Any questions?"

Kaleigh didn't know what to say. She didn't think that the split of the business was fair. She didn't exactly know what she thought the percentage would be but felt that it should have been closer to fifty-fifty.

All of a sudden Wesley began talking, "No, I think we are all set. Do we sign anything tonight?"

Dan walked over to his desk and answered, "Yes, let's get the bank account papers taken care of tonight. I imagine you two want some time to think about the business portion and if one of you is buying the other one out," Dan replied and began shuffling papers on his desk. "So we can wait a few weeks before we do anything with that."

Dan found the papers he was looking for, relating to Dad's accounts, and organized them on the table in front of them. Kaleigh found herself unable to speak. She didn't know what to say. The day she found her dad's shaky signature on the sign-in sheet flashed into her head. She looked up and noticed that Wesley had begun to sign his papers. Kaleigh's head started to spin. She was frozen in shock at this moment. Did Dad really think that she only deserved twenty percent of the business? Yes, these past few years, Wesley had done more to keep the Garden Center going, but she had stepped up too. She had done her part with Dad, taking care of things when he got hurt, helping more and putting things into place when things got more and more difficult for him at the house. Kaleigh put in hours of work when Dad needed to move to assisted living. It was her who worked with the realtor to sell the house, the furniture, moving so many things into her basement. All those hours of work on that end of things had to account for something. It was never really about the money. She was making a good living, but the outcome didn't seem fair. It was the lack of fairness in it all, not the money, that bothered her.

"Kaleigh . . . Kaleigh." It took a moment for her to realize that Dan had been calling her name as she came out of her fog. Her mind was just racing.

"Oh yes," she said, picking up a pen to sign. As she was signing, Wesley said, "I gotta go. Talk to you soon, Kaleigh." And just as quickly as he had come in, he was gone.

Kaleigh left the office with mixed emotions. She was sad that all of this meant that her dad was really gone. Then there was the nagging feeling that the split of the Garden Center wasn't fair at all. Was this what Dad really wanted? And why was Dad at the lawyer's office that day, now almost three months ago, when Kaleigh knew he was not able to drive or make any decisions at that point in his life?

Whenever there was a huge and confusing event that happened in Kaleigh's life, she dialed Danielle.

"Help!" Her voice was shaky as she called out to her friend as soon as she picked up the phone.

"What! What's wrong? Do you need me to come and meet you?" Danielle heard the desperation in her best friend's voice and knew it was serious.

"Yes, please, can you come over?" Kaleigh just wanted to be in her pajamas on her couch at this point.

"Absolutely, I'll bring the wine." Danielle had a feeling that the seriousness of the phone call and her friend's frantic voice meant that something was needed to calm the nerves.

At that point, Kaleigh realized how hungry she was and decided to stop at the sandwich place for some take-out for her and her best friend.

****

By the time Danielle arrived, Kaleigh was already in her pajamas and was unwrapping the sandwiches she had chosen.

"What happened?" were the first words out of Danielle's mouth after she put the bottle of wine on the counter and gave her friend a hug.

"Oh gosh, where to begin?" Her mind continued to race as she handed her friend a plate and offered her to choose a sandwich. Then Kaleigh opened and poured two glasses of wine.

After that, Kaleigh started going through all she had done these past few years for her dad when Wesley seemed to want nothing to do with anything outside the store. Danielle knew the story but knew that her friend had to work through everything in her brain and listened intently.

"I have helped at the Garden Center for as long as I can remember. It is just as much my legacy as it is Wesley's. I mean, yes, I had to step away when Dad's health took a turn, but I took care of Dad when Wes wouldn't, or couldn't. I never did ask him why he didn't help much with Dad. Someday, maybe I will figure that out."

Kaleigh paused for a moment, then continued, "And then, when Dan said that the Garden Center is to be split . . ." She paused a moment, then said, "eighty percent to Wes, twenty percent to me, I froze."

Between the two friends, there was silence. Danielle couldn't believe what she was hearing as much as Kaleigh couldn't believe that what she had just said was actually true.

Both took a sip of wine, and then Kaleigh continued, "What should I do? Is anything I can do?"

"There has to be." Danielle replied.

"Oh, I forgot to tell you! So, after Dad died, Wes kept saying he would call the lawyer's office to set up an appointment, but he never did. Days kept going by and still no word about an appointment with the lawyer. I decided to stop by and at least see about a life insurance policy—something that would help with the funeral home and final expenses. I figured that would be OK as I wasn't asking about the will yet. Anyway, the secretary had me sign in while I was waiting for her to finish with another client. I couldn't believe my eyes. As I was signing at the bottom of the sheet, I noticed Dad's very shaky signature on the top line of the paper, with a date of about two months before. That signature has been nagging at me ever since. Two months ago, when dad's mind wasn't clear and he wasn't able to drive, he was at the lawyer's office. How could that be? Why was he there? Who drove him? At that point he hadn't been driving in a long time." Kaleigh's heart was racing, and her head began to pound. She rubbed her head at that moment, and Danielle put her hand on her friend's shoulder as she got up to get her some medicine.

As Danielle returned to the couch with the medicine bottle, she shared her thoughts. "We know that jealousy, pain, and hurt, when bottled up, can cause people to do crazy things. Maybe this has something to do with Wesley, maybe not. Do we trust Dan and the team at his office to tell you the truth? Do you want to go down that road to find the answers? Or do you want to leave things alone?"

Those were all great questions.

"Was there anything else in the will?" Danielle continued.

"Just the money left in his bank account from the sale of the house and the garage sale I had. That gets split fifty-fifty." Kaleigh replied as she took another bite of her sandwich.

"Do you need the money?" Another good question from her best friend.

"No, it's not about the money. It is just the matter of fairness. I have done as much or almost as much extra work as Wesley has." After she spoke these words she rested her head on the back of the couch and closed her eyes for a moment.

"It's up to you. Do you want answers? Or do you want to leave things as they are?" Danielle continued with all the right questions.

Danielle realized she was giving her friend a lot to think about and that she should relax and let Kaleigh think. She grabbed her friend's hand and said, "Whatever you decide, I am here for you and will help you as much as I can."

Kaleigh gave her friend's hand a squeeze back and said, "Thank you."

She was not in the mood or the mindset to make any decisions tonight, but her friend did give her so many good things to think about.

CHAPTER 15

A few nights later, there was a storm. There hadn't been one in a while, but this was a big one. As Kaleigh sat up in bed, her heart racing, her thoughts went to what Jackson had said. It is one thing to have friends to help talk things through, but a therapist would be better at possibly making these nightmares end. She needed them to end.

The next morning, she messaged her doctor for a referral to a good therapist, and by the end of the day she had received a call from her doctor and they had had a conversation about what Kaleigh had been going through. She then gave Kaleigh a referral to a therapist she trusted. Even though she hadn't talked to Jackson in a while, she knew it was the right thing to follow his advice. It could only help.

A few more days had passed, and Kaleigh had spent some time really thinking about how to proceed with the will. One day after school, she caught Danielle in the staff room.

"Hey, can I get yours and Chris' opinion on what to do next about the will?" Kaleigh asked her best friend.

"Absolutely. When do you want to get together?" Danielle asked.

"What are you guys doing Saturday?" Kaleigh asked.

"Actually, Saturday is our anniversary. But we don't have plans until three o'clock. Wanna get some coffee earlier?" Danielle quickly added that option. She wanted to be there for her friend.

"Are you sure?" Kaleigh didn't want to cut into their special day.

"Not a problem at all. I am going to the salon at ten. Chris and I can meet you at one o'clock, if you don't mind him coming along."

Danielle knew that Chris would be fine with that plan. He liked Kaleigh, and they hadn't seen each other in a while. Chris was just as supportive as Danielle was and Kaleigh trusted his advice as much as Danielle's.

"Only if you're sure, I mean, it's your anniversary. You'd probably rather be somewhere else that day." Kaleigh replied.

"Absolutely, we will be there!" Danielle replied, giving her friend a hug on their way out.

****

While replaying the events in her mind, Kaleigh realized that if she had not seen the sign-in sheet at the lawyer's office, she might have felt OK leaving things as they were. There would not have been a glaring reason to question the division of the store. But she did see the signature. Even if she hadn't taken a picture that day, the shaky signature of her father would be forever etched in her mind. That was what was making it hard to just let the uneven ownership of the Garden Center go.

The idea of Danielle going to a salon made Kaleigh think that she was due for some pampering of her own. On Friday night after work, she stopped at the nail salon and got a manicure and pedicure. Then the next morning, she went to get her hair done at an inexpensive salon in town. She wanted a refresh and was hoping it would make her feel stronger and better about this crazy situation she was in.

When she met Danielle and Chris for coffee, she felt good. The refresh was way overdue as she couldn't remember the last time she had her hair done. Kaleigh was never one to spend a lot of money on her beauty routine. She was always a believer in the idea that less is more, but this refresh really felt so good. With all the heartache lately, she needed a boost.

Her friends had gotten to the coffee shop first. When Kaleigh arrived, she noticed that they were already seated at a table. After stopping at the counter to put her order in, she joined her them at the quiet table in the corner.

It had been a while since the three of them had time to relax and catch up. Chris had a job with a tech company and often traveled across the country. He and Danielle had not had any children yet, but growing their family was definitely in their future. Danielle felt so lucky to have Kaleigh, as it gave her a friend to lean on, especially when her husband was out of town.

After catching Kaleigh up on his company and all the amazing things they were doing, Chris asked the big question. "So, what's going on with you, Kaleigh?"

For a moment, she stared at her coffee, which had been delivered to the table during their conversation. Then she began. She shared with him everything that she had told Danielle last week, starting from her Saturdays at the Garden Center while she was teaching full-time. She continued to describe her dad's declining ability to take care of himself, the move to Assisted Living, and the subsequent sale of the house, furniture and many of his belongings. As for the doctor's appointments, Kaleigh had taken Dad to as many as she could, only asking Wesley for help when it was truly necessary. There were many conversations she had with his doctors via phone or messaging as she worked to make sure that Dad had everything he needed to stay healthy. Kaleigh reminded the two of them that, Wesley did not lift much of a finger when it came to Dad, for the move, the sale of the house, or the funeral. It wasn't for lack of trying. Kaleigh asked Wesley for help throughout each transitional period and consistently received the response, "I can't, I'm just really busy." Aside from Wesley going with Dad to the occasional doctor's appointment, it was Kaleigh who did everything for their dad. Kaleigh never complained about it. She just did what needed to be done. She also shared that, during all of these changes, Wesley's attitudes and actions continued to change. As the years and months had gone on, it was as if he was crawling into a shell, pulling farther away from their little family, and no longer the humorous, fun-loving brother he once was. Looking back now, Kaleigh could see how truly different her brother was now.

After taking another sip of coffee, she told Chris about the sign-in sheet at the lawyer's office, the outcome of the will, and Wesley's behavior that entire week. He was shocked. He wasn't sure what to say at first, so he just let the information set in as he took a sip of his coffee. Danielle didn't say a word, as she knew when to stay quiet and let things sink in.

Then, after a quiet few moments Kaleigh added, "And I want to fight it."

Chris, setting his coffee down, replied, "I think you should."

Danielle, who was listening and watching her friend intently the entire time, added, "Yes, you should, and we will do what we can to help."

"That's the thing." Kaleigh continued, placing her hands around the warm cup in front of her, "I don't know where to begin, where to go, who can help me." Kaleigh was speaking now in a worried tone.

"Let me call my friend Johnathan. He is a friend of mine from college and lives about forty minutes away. He is a lawyer in Stevensville. I mean, I don't know if he himself can take your case, but he has to know someone who can. This type of predicament must happen to people, right? I mean the lies, the deception of trying to change someone's will." Although Chris had known a few deceptive people throughout his life, he had never encountered someone who had gone to such great lengths to deceive, to lie, and to cheat another person out of money from a will.

Kaleigh wanted to ask the question, the one that had been stuck in the back of her mind all week. But it was Chris who alluded to it, which gave her the courage to ask it out loud. "So . . . you think Wes is behind this?"

"Absolutely," he replied without hesitation. "I mean, the stars, the facts, the behavior, it all lines up. Wesley continues to pull back from the family as he is forced to take more responsibility at the store. He refuses to help most times when you need him, loses his kind nature. You shared how he keeps to himself, stops any form of deep conversation and how, on some days, won't have one at all. He moves nervously whenever you bring up the lawyer's office, won't even call them. Then avoided the lawyers office at first, and, when he does show up, signs quick and leaves as fast as he came in. But to me, it's your dad's shaky signature that puts the icing on the cake. Yes, absolutely I think Wesley is to blame."

The three stayed quiet for a minute. Chris and Danielle knew that it was a lot for Kaleigh to take in. It was hard to hear that her brother might be to blame.

Danielle reached across the table to gently grab her friends' hand and give it a squeeze, as if to say, "We are with you in this." Then Kaleigh found herself saying, "I'm sorry."

Immediately Danielle responded, "What are you apologizing for? We are the ones that dropped a lot on you to think about," Danielle said, still holding her friend's hand.

"It's your anniversary, and you are taking the time to help me with this mess. I am ruining your day." Kaleigh said as she let out a sigh.

"Danielle was about to say something but Chris beat her to it, "You are doing no such thing. You gave us something to do. Otherwise we would've been all dressed up just staring at each other from across the couch!" They all chuckled before Danielle chimed in, "We want to help you."

"Thank you, I really appreciate you both!" Kaleigh replied, grateful more than ever now for their friendship.

"I will text Johnathan tomorrow and let you know what I find out. We will find someone to investigate this." Chris said as he looked at Kaleigh, making sure she knew that he was behind her, that they would support her through everything.

"I really appreciate it. I mean, if I didn't have the picture of Dad's shaky signature in my head . . . if I hadn't seen it, then maybe I would feel differently about all this. Maybe I could let it go. But I can't. I can't let it go." Kaleigh fought back the tears.

"You have a picture of the signature, don't you?" Danielle reminded her friend.

"Oh yes," Kaleigh said as she pulled out her phone and scrolled through the photos. It wasn't long before she was showing the two the photo she had taken at the lawyer's office that day.

"We've got this," Chris said. "I mean, Johnathan, or one of his buddies, has this!"

The last comment, and the feeling of support she was feeling in this moment caused Kaleigh to relax a bit and smile. They stayed for another hour, talking about other things, less stressful topics, and just enjoying each other's company. It felt good to be with friends and talk over a cup of coffee. It had been a while since she was able to relax so freely. Danielle and Chris were celebrating their five-year wedding anniversary and had plans for the rest of the evening, but

Kaleigh was grateful that they had allowed her to be a part of their day. She gave them each a great big hug on their way out of the shop.

Afterwards, Kaleigh decided to go grocery shopping. She brought with her a list of items she needed to begin her quest to see if she was a good cook and a great baker like her mom. She was feeling a bit stronger in this moment, with the thought of her friends having her back, though there was still a sadness, a hole in her heart.

On her way home, Kaleigh drove past Rita's and her mind turned immediately to Jackson. She still hadn't heard from him. She remembered what Danielle had said, to give him some time and then write to him, explain everything. And that was what she did. That night, over a glass of wine, sitting in her kitchen, she wrote:

> *Dear Jackson,*
>
> *I am sorry for everything I have done. It seems I may have lost you as a friend, and this breaks my heart. That night that we were supposed to go to dinner, I had gotten home, and Jeremy had surprised me and was at my door. I mean, he told me he wanted to come for the funeral, but that was all that was said. I wasn't expecting him to come so soon.*
>
> *Jeremy is only a friend, and I should have spent more time with you the week of Dad's funeral. I regret that I didn't. You haven't answered my messages so I am guessing that I must have pushed you away. I didn't mean to push you away. I need you back in my life. I need my friend back, and I am truly sorry for any pain I may have caused you.*
>
> *With all my heart,*
> *Kaleigh*

On Monday, she mailed the letter on her way to work.

****

On Monday afternoon, she received a phone call from Johnathan. The number that came up on her phone was one she did not recognize, though something told her to answer it.

"Hello," Kaleigh answered.

"Hello, is this Kaleigh?" The voice on the other line was that of a man with a nice, personable voice.

"Yes, it is," she replied. "How can I help you?"

"This is Johnathan, Chris's friend from college. I'm a lawyer in Stevensville. Chris said you might need some help with a predicament regarding your father's will."

"Oh yes, thank you for calling." Kaleigh replied, thinking, "Wow, that was fast!"

"Do you have time to talk now, or should we set up another time?" Johnathan continued, seeming very nice on the other end of the phone. It was a gentle and helpful tone, not rushed as she suspected lawyers often were. And for him to call, and not his secretary, that seemed different, special.

"Um . . ." Realizing she needed to answer him, she continued, "Yes, I can talk now. Let me just walk out to my car. I'm just leaving school." As she said this, she began quickly putting some papers and her computer in her bag. Scanning her desk for what she had forgotten she reached for her lunch bag, then her coffee cup and started walking out of her classroom.

"Oh, you're a teacher?" Johnathan asked. And they continued talking with small talk until Kaleigh was settled in her car.

"OK," Kaleigh began, "How much time do you have? It's a story with a lot of parts to it."

"I'm OK on time. Let me hear it," Johnathan replied.

So, for the next ten minutes, Kaleigh shared her story, reflecting on and remembering all she had done for her father and the store throughout the years. Then she told of Wesley's, including how he had changed in the years that Dad's health was fading. Then, finally, she got to the events surrounding the lawyer's office.

Johnathan was quiet for a moment. Then he said, "Wow, you really have a lot of great information there. Yes, I do think you have grounds to file papers to question the will. There is definitely enough to make a real case here. I can help you if you would you like to proceed. Have you thought about whether you would like to officially question the will?"

"Yes, I mean, it is not about the money for me, but I know that this wasn't my father's wishes for the Garden Center, for his legacy. And the fact that I saw my dad's shaky signature in the lawyer's office, that picture that I will never get out of my mind, makes me certain about this. So, yes, I would like to file the papers." Kaleigh was more sure than ever, especially now that she had spoken to a lawyer who agreed that there was a case.

"OK." Johnathan then went over the next steps and assured her that only he would be taking on this investigation, with just one of his secretaries having any knowledge of the case, helping with some of the paperwork related to the investigation. He assured her that this investigation would be a quiet one so as not to draw attention from anyone. He also said that he works carefully so as not to land the story in the local papers. Kaleigh appreciated that so much. It would be Johnathan visiting Dan's office, Havenwood, and the doctor's office, collecting the necessary information. He shared with Kaleigh that he would need some signatures from her before he could fully begin the tasks ahead.

"Can you meet me for coffee on Saturday morning? I can come to you." Johnathan asked, really seeming ready and willing to take this on. And since he was a friend of Chris's, she knew she could trust him.

"Absolutely," she replied. They agreed to text during the week to confirm the time for Saturday. Kaleigh told him how grateful she was for his help and his time, and they ended the call.

Kaleigh felt better now and decided to call Danielle and Chris that night to let them know she had spoken with Johnathan. She shared how reassured she felt about the quiet investigation that would happen and how only he and his secretary would know of the case at all. She thanked them multiple times during the conversation as she felt grateful and blessed to have their help and support.

****

Jackson had gotten Kaleigh's letter with his mail on Tuesday. He stared at it every day, leaving it on his kitchen counter, unopened, for days. Sometimes he would hold it in his hand; other times, he would just stop to look at it for a second, then walk away. He didn't know what it would say, why she wrote to him. He was partly scared, partly intrigued.

By Friday night, he decided it was time. He built a fire in the fireplace, brought his dinner and a drink to the couch, and held the letter in his hand. He looked at her handwriting. Then slowly and carefully, opened the envelope, pulled out the note, and unfolded it. There was Kaleigh's beautiful handwriting. As he read the words his heart began to warm. The jealousy that he had in his heart for the past few weeks he could feel slowly melting away as he read what she had taken the time to write. Maybe there was hope yet. Maybe he wouldn't have to let her go. These past few weeks had been rough on him, trying, but unable to get her out of his mind. Deep down, he knew that he should trust Kaleigh, as she had never lied to him. Jeremy was a friend from college—he knew that—but when Kaleigh leaned on him that week of the funeral instead of him and when she had forgotten the plans they had, it really stung. Now, looking at the words she wrote—still wanting to be friends, missing him—warmed his heart and began to chip away at the jealousy and sadness he had been feeling. He was happy to have some hope return to his heart.

Jackson did not always go to the coffee shop, but on occasion he would stop by. The next morning, Jackson decided to go. These past few weeks he had avoided going into town on the weekends, as the thought of seeing her or running into her would be too painful. He thought it best to keep his distance.

But that morning, the morning after reading her letter, was different. He wanted to run into her, to see her, talk to her. He wanted to tell her how much he appreciated her letter. More than anything he wanted to spend time with her again, like they used to. He missed her deeply, and as much as he thought he could let her go and move on with his life, as the days passed by, he realized that was going to be impossible. He didn't want to text her. Jackson was always under the mindset that talking to someone in person was much better than a text. He was really hoping to run into her.

There wasn't a close parking spot that morning, but Jackson didn't mind the walk. He didn't know if she would be there, but he thought he would try. Maybe if she wasn't there, he would bring her coffee, like he did that morning so long ago. Not sure what his exact plan was, he took his time, walking the sidewalk of shops on the way to the coffee shop, which was the last business down on the right. When he got closer, he noticed Kaleigh sitting outside at a table. Her back was to him, but he knew it was her. And there, sitting across from her, was a gentleman in a suit, nonetheless. Then, at that moment, Jackson's fragile heart, which had lifted its spirit just hours before with the words in Kaleigh's letter, had his heart sink back down into his stomach once more. He immediately turned around and walked away. His original plan, to let her go, seemed to be the only one left at this point. Jackson didn't know who the man was, but he was shocked to see her with a man. Who was that? What was she doing talking to a man in a suit? His heart was racing a bit as he walked back toward his car. Maybe he would just have to keep avoiding her, and maybe, someday, his heart would heal.

Jackson had no idea what was going on in Kaleigh's life. And why would he? Danielle and Chris were the only ones who knew what was going on, and even if they were friends with Jackson, which they weren't, they wouldn't tell him. She trusted her friends dearly and knew that they would keep this matter to themselves.

That morning at the coffee shop, Johnathan had gotten there first and was seated at a table outside. It was a beautiful day. He had a small folder with him, which was sitting on the table next to him as Kaleigh walked up. After figuring out that the man was, in fact, Johnathan, she ran to grab a cup of coffee and came back to sit across from him.

They spoke for about thirty minutes, and Johnathan took more detailed notes. Then, after Kaleigh showed him the photograph of the sign-in sheet and sent it to him, all that was left was to sign the papers officially making Johnathan her lawyer. Kaleigh signed the official petition questioning the will that he would file at the state probate court, and then one more paper giving him permission to speak to various people in his efforts to investigate the case.

Upon leaving the coffee shop, Kaleigh felt a weird sense of calm. Johnathan had gone over the next steps and told her that it would be a few weeks before they would need to meet again but that in the meantime he would do the digging he needed to get the necessary proof they needed to right the wrong. He would call if he needed anything and would let her know when he had a court date. He also said that, in the meantime, she should relax and continue living her life as normal. And that, if possible, she should stay away from the lawyer's office. If she needed anything from that office, she should make a quick phone call or contact Johnathan, and he would take care of it. Kaleigh thanked him again and again, as she was just so grateful for his amazing help in all of this.

CHAPTER 16

It would be a couple of weeks before she would hear any more from Johnathan. In the meantime, Kaleigh kept busy with the end-of-the-school-year grading, projects, events, and organization that came with wrapping up another school year. She was at a concert, a play, or a staff party every other night for two weeks straight, and she was tired.

In addition to the business of another school year wrapping up, she had started meeting with her new therapist and had begun to feel better about taking this step. They had decided to begin with one meeting per week to start, and then after a few weeks, they might be able to meet a bit less.

Kaleigh felt good sharing with an impartial person the events of her childhood. She spoke about the closeness she was lucky to have with both of her parents, the tragic loss of her mother, and the loss of her father, all which happened way too soon.

She replayed the night, years earlier, hopefully retelling it for the last time. On the night of the crash, the phone had rung at the house after nine o'clock. Dad had answered the phone and Kaleigh could remember the vision so clearly, her dad sinking into the kitchen chair, his head falling into his hand. A few minutes later the investigator rang the doorbell and dad went out on the front porch to talk to him. Kaleigh had felt compelled by something that night to join her father on the porch. She listened to the investigator as he went over everything that happened just an hour before, on a dark and wet back country road. As the officer spoke, there was a rumble of thunder and a bolt of lightning, as if to remind her that a storm had rolled through. It was difficult for Kaleigh to realize at that moment she would never see her mother again. Those graphic details that the investigator shared, of how, where and when the accident occurred were what had crept into her dreams. It was those feelings, those memories that Kaleigh and her therapist would work on unpacking and releasing as the weeks and months went by. Even after just two sessions, Kaleigh felt like progress was being made.

It was after these two exhausting weeks that she found herself staying in her jammies a little longer on that Saturday morning. She had made herself coffee, put a movie on the television, and grabbed her computer so that she could finish entering the final grades for her students' report cards. Kaleigh was truly ready for a quiet day at home when, suddenly, the doorbell rang.

The sound startled her at first, but then, the thought of maybe the visitor being Jackson made her heart perk up. Maybe he had gotten her letter and was here to see her. When she opened the door, she was startled, a little bewildered, and surprised to see who it was.

Lola, her cousin whom she had not seen in many years, was standing there on her porch, holding a baby. Well, a little person, old enough to hold herself up as Lola held the child on her hip.

Realizing that she was taking a long time for words to come out of her mouth, she stuttered for a second and then finally said, "Lola, oh my gosh, it's been so long. What are you doing here? Please"—she opened the door further—"come in."

Lola came inside and immediately gave her cousin a hug. "Why, who is this?" Kaleigh asked as she put her hand gently on the child's arm.

Lola was happy to be in the company of her cousin. She had been through a lot these past few months. Too much had happened for her to stay where she was, with no support system, and she was looking for a change. She realized she wasn't the best at returning messages lately and these last two days she had found herself driving to an address she got from Kaleigh's latest Christmas card.

"This is Hannah," Lola began. "She is nine months old. Her birthday is in September."

Kaleigh wanted to ask a million questions, like how she got here, what she had been doing these past few years, and more questions about Hannah, who, at this point, was crawling on the floor, looking like she needed something to play with. Kaleigh, not having any baby toys in the house, knew she had a teddy bear sitting on a chair in the guest bedroom and went to grab it.

When she returned to the room, she found herself sitting on the floor, moving the teddy bear and getting Hannah to crawl toward it. All the while, the little girl was giggling and laughing.

Lola had a smile on her face as she watched her cousin be so wonderful with her daughter. When a tear came to her eye she quickly wiped it away before Kaleigh noticed. After getting a drink for the two of them, something fizzy that she always had on hand to help calm the stomach and nerves, Kaleigh began to ask what was swirling around in her head.

"So, what are you doing here? I mean, I am so happy you came, but I had no idea you were coming. I would have gotten dressed this morning! And I had no idea you had a beautiful baby girl! She is just precious." Kaleigh didn't have to try with her voice at all. She was truly happy the two had come to visit and Lola could here this in the genuine tone in her voice. Lola settled more comfortably onto the couch, and began.

"Well, this is always difficult to say. The story of these past few months is the hardest that I have been through. I sent you a photo when Ryan and I got married. We were so happy, but his parents didn't approve of the marriage. They wanted him to finish college first and become a doctor. He wanted to be a counselor for kids. To tell you the truth, I don't think they wanted him to marry me at all, like I wasn't good enough, but they used him finishing college as an excuse. Oh, Kaleigh, he was so good with kids. You should have seen him. He was going to be an amazing counselor."

Kaleigh was intrigued and saddened all at the same time. "So, what happened?" she asked, wanting to hear more.

"It was about a year ago when Ryan started feeling excruciating pain. We thought it was the stomach bug, and he stayed in bed for a few days, but nothing changed and nothing we did seemed to help. If anything, the pain seemed to be getting worse. I was six months pregnant. I didn't know what else to do, so I called the ambulance and they took him to the hospital. They were able to dull the pain a little, but there wasn't much they could do. It was cancer. It had gotten him, and so fast. He was able to come home in July but was on so much medication. I tried to contact his parents to tell them, but they wouldn't return any of my calls, messages, notes, or anything. Hannah Hailey was born on September first. I called a neighbor to look after Ryan while I was in the hospital. I came home on the fourth without Hannah, as she was having some trouble breathing. She spent ten days in the NICU to strengthen her lungs."

At this point, the tears were streaming down Lola's face, and Kaleigh ran to the bathroom to get tissues. When she returned, Lola wiped her tears and continued.

"It wasn't until the fourteenth when I could bring Hannah home, and by that time, Ryan was so weak he could barely hold her, but he did, and the smile on his face, I will never forget it." She paused for a moment, wiped her eyes again, then said slowly, as it was still hard for her to speak the truth out loud, "He died two days later."

Lola sat there, wiping the tears that refused to stop, trying to compose herself. Kaleigh grabbed a tissue in this moment, as she could not longer hold back her tears. She didn't know what to say. It all seemed too much for one person to handle.

"Where are you living now?" Kaleigh asked.

"We are kind of in-between places right now. I ended up selling the house Ryan had bought for us, which paid for most of the medical bills. My parents, when they died last year, left me a little something, which got me through till now, but it seems I am at a fork in the road. I don't know what to do next. I don't have anyone. I got in the car and found myself here at your door. I'm sorry I didn't call."

"No, no, that's OK," Kaleigh replied as she got up to give her cousin a hug and wipe the hair from her face.

"You must be hungry. Would you like something to eat?" Kaleigh was suddenly grateful she had taken the time to look up recipes and buy some groceries in the last week. Her cooking was surprisingly good, and she found that she enjoyed doing it.

"That would be great!" Lola replied.

"Did you bring anything for Hannah? Do you have bags in the car we should get?" Kaleigh was hoping she had some toys for her to play with, to occupy her, as playing with the bear was getting old.

"Oh yes, I do have some things. Would it be OK if we stayed here for a little while? I mean, it's okay if you say no . . ." Kaleigh interrupted, "Nonsense, I wouldn't dream of it. You can absolutely stay here." And a moment later, Lola was holding Hannah, and the three went outside to get the bags out of the car. There was a small highchair that belted to a kitchen stool perfectly and some toys Hannah seemed to enjoy playing with. This allowed the two cousins time to cook together a delicious chicken parmesan and pasta. Hannah enjoyed eating the small pasta noodles, picking it up with her fingers, and shoving it in her mouth, missing about half of the time! The two cousins were laughing and snapping photos of this fun moment. Once Hannah wiped her pasta hands up to her eyes in tiredness, the two realized she needed a clean-up and a nap. Lola asked if she could use her bathroom, and Kaleigh showed her where her guest bedroom and bathroom were. Then she went out to Lola's car to find the travel bed Hannah had been using and set it up in Lola's new bedroom.

Kaleigh left the two alone for a while she tidied up the kitchen. When Lola came back, the two finished eating and then cleaned up the mess.

When they finally sat down on the couch with a cup of coffee, Kaleigh asked, "So what do you need? What can I do for you and Hannah?"

Lola, who was extremely grateful, began, "Well, I needed to leave our home. It was too painful to stay there, and I couldn't afford it. I stayed with a neighbor for a while, but when her son came home from college I knew we couldn't stay there any longer. I thought it would be good for Hannah and me to start over somewhere. I just don't know where that will be. I need some time to figure things out and a little help with Hannah so that I can try to find the new me, a new job, a place to live." There was a pause before Lola continued, "I mean, I know this is a lot to ask, but I couldn't think of anyone else. I don't have any other family, and Ryan's family continues to keep their distance. I didn't hear anything from his parents even after his death, so there was no service, just a burial with a prayer by a local pastor."

"I'm so sorry, Lola, for everything you have been through. I wish I had known sooner. I could have helped you move, came to visit, or sent you things." Kaleigh really did wish that she had known all the heartache her sweet cousin had been going through.

"I'm the one who should be sorry. I should have answered you sooner when you told me about your father's passing. I did love him. I just think my heart was too raw after all that had happened. I just couldn't bear coming to a funeral, but I should have replied. I'm so sorry Kaleigh." Lola truly regretted not texting her cousin back weeks ago. Especially when she had been so nice to offer help.

"Oh, Lola, there is nothing to be sorry about. We all heal in our own ways. You had so much going on and needed to focus on that beautiful girl you have. I completely understand." And the two embraced in another hug.

For the next hour, they talked about everything that Kaleigh had been going through, minus the parts about Jackson and Jeremy and the will. Then they made a list of things that Lola and Hannah would need to be comfortable living here for a little while. Kaleigh was happy that she was almost on summer vacation so that she could help her cousin. She was happy to help her cousin figure out what her next steps would be. And not because it would be a good diversion away from the trouble with the will, her brother, and her missing friend, Jackson. Though the detour away from her troubles was a welcome one.

The grocery list was the most important, as Hannah needed some of her favorites to have in the house for when she was hungry. They decided they would go to the store once Hannah woke from her nap. When Kaleigh woke up this morning she had a completely different plan, but she was very happy with how the day turned out. The company and someone else for her to worry about was good for Kaleigh. She had spent the last couple of weeks dwelling on her life and its events when the events of her sweet cousin's life this past year were so much more tragic. It helped Kaleigh put her life into perspective.

Chapter 17

There was just one more week left of school that day when Lola knocked on her door. Kaleigh didn't get to her grading that weekend, as her focus had quickly changed to making sure Lola and Hannah had everything they needed. This meant a stop at a couple of stores when Hannah awoke from her nap. By dinner time, they had a toy area set up for the baby, the refrigerator was full, and Lola and Kaleigh were relaxing with a salad in the family room.

The two had decided that they would see how the summer went and that Kaleigh would help with Hannah so that Lola could try to figure out where she might get a job, where she might find a place to live, and all in all, what her new normal might look like. Kaleigh was excited for the company. She was hoping this would help her not feel so alone this summer, as she still had not heard from Jackson, and with each day that went by, she had became more sad and discouraged over losing her friend. Kaleigh hoped that this new family dynamic would keep her spirits up and be a nice distraction from her troubles.

That week was long, with evenings spent on her computer, finishing up report card grades and comments after she had spent an extra hour after school daily cleaning out and cleaning up her room. She always covered her shelves and cleaned off her desk so that her items were out of the way for the custodians, who always had projects and cleaning to do over the summer. There were usually a lot of items that found their way to the recycle bins as she tidied up her files to stay organized. The deadlines were looming, but it always was a fun and exciting week! This school year, with everything she had been through, seemed so very long. Lola did sweet things around the house for Kaleigh, as she wanted her to know how much she appreciated her.

The eighth-grade picnic was Thursday afternoon at the park behind the school. The teachers and parents helped to set up the event, including fun games all along the winding path that connected the school to the park. Each year the theme was luau and it always made for such an amazing way to say goodbye to the students. Kaleigh always stayed to help clean up and had invited Lola and Hannah to come once the buses took the student's home. Hannah was not quite taking her first steps yet, so Lola had her in the stroller. Between the bubble machine and the balloons, Hannah stayed happy as everyone bustled around to clean up after the event.

Kaleigh introduced Lola to Danielle, as the two hadn't had a chance to meet. They appreciated her help and had fun making Hannah laugh too. Toward the end of clean-up, Danielle asked if she could hold the baby, walked her around the park, and then took her to the baby swing. Lola appreciated the break as much as the two appreciated her help. By the time they were finished, Danielle had invited Lola and Hannah to come to dinner along with Kaleigh tomorrow night.

Danielle and Kaleigh made it a tradition to go out for a nice dinner together to celebrate the final day of the school year. Chris came as well, and it was a wonderful way to close out the year. Lola appreciated being invited, and Hannah made the evening fun as she was such a happy baby. After the drinks came, Danielle cleared her throat gently to gain everyone's attention, raised her glass and said, "Here is to another great year! Here's to those we have lost," (she paused and looked at Kaleigh), "those we have found," (she paused to look at Lola), "and those who are on the way!" And at that moment, she touched her belly and looked at Kaleigh for her reaction.

Kaleigh took a second to register what her friend meant, then said, "Really, are you pregnant?" in what came out as an excited squeal. Danielle smiled and nodded while Kaleigh continued, "Oh my gosh, you are going to be the best mom!" she said, then jumped up to give the parents-to-be a hug saying, "Congratulations!" And when the waitress returned, Danielle quickly traded her glass of wine for a ginger ale.

They talked for a while about the baby, which was due in December. They spoke of vacations. Chris and Danielle were taking their final big vacation before becoming parents, and Kaleigh and Danielle would drive to the coast for a few days toward the end of summer. Danielle said she didn't want to miss out on this last trip with her best friend before the baby came. The big project this summer would be to change the guest bedroom into a nursery and make the basement suitable for guests. While Chris was pretty handy, he still planned on calling in some help for the big tasks.

Lola fit right into the conversation. She really was personable and fun and had good stories to tell. When the group spoke about the nursery, Lola gave the soon-to-be parents some great ideas of what they would need for the baby's room, as well as notes about items that everyone buys but aren't really necessary Then the conversation turned to what Lola thought she wanted to do in this next stage of her life. She told them how much she loved working with kids, so she planned on going to daycare centers and schools to see what jobs might be available. It would be difficult to work elsewhere, she figured, as she would need care for Hannah. At least at a daycare center, she could bring the baby with her. She was going to begin looking for work this week. Danielle offered to help watch Hannah whenever Kaleigh couldn't, and Lola was very appreciative. Both Kaleigh and Lola offered to help with the work Danielle and Chris had to do at their house this summer, and all of this made Kaleigh happy. She was grateful to have a family again with Lola and Hannah and to have best friends who were growing theirs! It would be a great summer.

****

Jackson's farm and all his business ventures continued to keep him busy and bring in a lot of money. He was always good with money and balanced his finances so that he could afford to hire good help instead of being stuck with having to do everything himself. He stayed busy with work but also found himself going a bit stir-crazy when he wasn't on the job. The house he lived in was minimal, cozy, and cute. He didn't fill the house with any more than he needed but did have a guest bedroom and bathroom, which was used by his cousin who sometimes came into town.

On days when he couldn't seem to sit still, he found himself going for long walks on and around his property. Then one day, he ended up going for a long jog up the hill and down the road past where his farm ended. It was like he needed to get off the property to clear his head. He still didn't know what his next step should be with Kaleigh. He continued to miss her dearly and realized that getting over her was harder than he ever thought it would be. Maybe he wasn't supposed to get over her. Maybe in the end, they were supposed to be together. He never was a runner in all his life, but lately, on days when he was home and feeling antsy, this was what he did. During these long jogs, he would work many different plans through his head, hoping that one day, one plan that he came up with for him and Kaleigh would make sense. He continue to hope that, one day, what he was supposed to do would just come to him and feel right. The jogs took him at least two miles down the road before he would turn around. When he returned home, he would shower and feel more relaxed, less keyed-up, and less stressed. Jogging was his new coping mechanism.

If Jackson hadn't known about Kaleigh's nightmares on stormy nights, maybe it would have been easier to move on and not think about her so much. But he did know. And on every stormy night, he found himself wondering if she was OK. He imagined her waking up startled, breathing heavily, and doing her best to calm down as she realized it was just a dream. He wondered if she had decided to talk to someone, a therapist, who could help her get past these nightmares.

Kaleigh would often think of Jackson too. She wondered what he was doing and how he was doing. She felt that the next move should be his, as she wrote the letter and hadn't gotten no response. Too much time had passed to begin a text to him now. It was becoming clear to her that he wasn't interested and that she had to continue keeping her distance. If after reading her note, he still didn't want to be friends, she would have to accept that. It would be a very sad reality for her to come to terms with, that maybe their paths were not supposed to cross again. Maybe their relationship, even just as friends, wasn't meant to be.

Kaleigh had yet to bring up Jackson to her therapist, though she was sure that it would come up soon enough. Jackson was such a key part of her story—"was" being the keyword. At least she had the company of Lola and Hannah to help bring a light to her life. It cut the sadness of missing her best friend down a little. There was nothing that could take the sadness completely away, but her new family was definitely helping her cope, giving her something positive in her life.

****

The first Sunday of summer, while Lola and Hannah were home, Kaleigh decided to run some errands in the middle of the day. She stopped at the liquor store, then the discount store for some more plant food, and finally, the grocery store. When she pulled into a spot in the grocery store parking lot, she heard a text come through and took a moment to check. It was Lola asking her if she could pick up something for the baby that she had forgotten. When Kaleigh finished the reply, she looked up and saw him. Her heart skipped a beat. Jackson was walking out of the store, and carrying two bags to his truck. His hair was shorter. He was wearing jeans, rugged boots, and a tight T-shirt. He looked really good, and at that moment, her heart sank, suddenly feeling heavy. Sitting in her car, after not seeing him for so long, she felt a lump deep in her chest. It was a horrible feeling that she could not shake. One that would remain there for the rest of the day, even when she lay in bed later that night, trying so hard to just fall asleep.

Kaleigh had so many thoughts swimming through her mind. First, she thought, "I miss him so much." Then, the next moment brought the question, "How do I fix this?" "What if he truly doesn't want me in his life anymore?" Then came the realization, "I don't think I can live without Jackson." And finally, she thought, "I don't want to." She wasn't sure what to do. What could she do? The letter didn't work, and he was most likely avoiding her because they didn't run into each other in town anymore. They hadn't seen each other in months. She would have to think of something, some way to talk to him, to tell him how she felt. But when would be a good time? How would she tell him? She would have to think of something. But for now, she had a family to help take care of.

It was at that moment that Kaleigh realized she needed to pull herself together. She ran her fingers through her hair and checked her complexion in the mirror. By this time Jackson had pulled away. She grabbed her phone, keys, and purse and went into the store.

****

Now that school had ended and Kaleigh had finished the last of the organization and cleaning out of her classroom, she finally began her summer. She spent a few days working outside in her yard, cleaning it up, trimming, planting new flowers, and adding fresh mulch. This was the one time she went to the local discount store instead of her dad's—well, her and Wesley's—Garden Center. Wow, this was the first time she had thought of the store as hers and Wesley's. The first time she had caught herself not calling it, Dad's store. As she worked in her yard, she decided she would always think of the Garden Center as Dad's store. It was weird being in another garden store, but at this point it was necessary.

A few days later, Kaleigh got a call from Johnathan.

"Hi, Kaleigh. Do you have time to talk?" he began. "I have some news."

"Of course," she replied.

"So, I finished my research, and I know we have the proof we need." Johnathan was excited to give her the news, and it showed in his voice.

"Wow, what did you find out?" Kaleigh asked.

"Well, it turns out Wesley did pick your dad up from Havenwood that day and drove him to the lawyer's office. He and your dad met with Dan, and I have proof that the will was changed that day. It had originally read that the Garden Center would be split fifty-fifty until that day when Wesley got your dad to change the will." Johnathan had spent the last few weeks collecting information, facts, interview truths, and signatures from everyone from the doctor, the staff at Havenwood, the secretary at the lawyer's office, and Dan himself. He had left no stone unturned and had all the proof they needed.

"Wow, I . . . I don't know what to say, but thank you," Kaleigh was stunned and shocked, even though in the back of her mind, Chris and Danielle had said that might be the case, that Wesley was most likely to blame. She knew it could be a possibility, but it was still hard to swallow that her brother could have, would have, done this.

"You are very welcome. You were right to question the will, and I know that we will win. I am just going to need a couple more signatures from you, and then I will take my findings to the court. The court will reach out to Wes to see if he would like to fight this or settle outside of court." Johnathan wanted to make sure Kaleigh understood what the next steps would be, but he wondered, "Have you talked to Wesley at all?"

"No, I just don't know what to say. I didn't know if he knew what was happening, that I was investigating the will. He hasn't called me either." Kaleigh replied.

"Well, he will know now, so be prepared. He may call you." Johnathan wanted to make sure she was prepared for whatever may happen. "You don't have to talk to him, but if you do, keep it simple and let him know that things can be settled in or out of court— that it is his choice." His words were very reassuring and kind.

Before the two hung up the phone, they decided to meet the day after tomorrow, again at the coffee shop. Kaleigh would sign the papers, and the rest would be up to Wesley and the judge. Johnathan would be with her every step of the way, and Kaleigh shared how grateful she was for that as they ended the conversation.

CHAPTER 18

There were a few stormy nights in between Kaleigh's meetings with the therapist. Most nights, she did wake up with the nightmare, but one morning she had finally slept through a storm. Kaleigh never really paid much attention to the weather in terms of when storms might happen. The only reason she figured out that she had slept through a storm was what she noticed out her kitchen window as she poured herself some coffee. Through the large raindrops on the kitchen window, she saw a branch across the street that had fallen off the neighbor's tree. Looking at the recent radar on her phone, she saw that at 5:00 a.m., sure enough, a thunderstorm had rolled through. She let out a sigh and thought maybe the therapy sessions were getting somewhere. She had actually slept right through this storm

Kaleigh was happy with her therapist and did feel stronger and more confident now that she was able to get the heavy weight of her memories, her story, off her chest. Her therapist was amazing. She was the kind of therapist that knew when to stay quiet, when to ask questions, and knew what to say in such a caring, understanding way. Kaleigh could feel that her time with the therapist was making a difference but wasn't sure if the nightmares would ever be able to completely disappear for good. That morning, she was excited to think that maybe there was hope.

****

Lola had been motivated to look for a job in her quest to start her life over. She was not the type of person who would take advantage of her cousin for very long or overstay her welcome. On the day that Kaleigh had planned to meet Johnathan to sign the papers, Lola had already scheduled an interview at a daycare center in a neighboring town and needed someone to watch Hannah. Kaleigh did not mind watching the baby at all and thought it would be fun to take her into town. She loaded the car seat, the baby, and her stroller into the car, and then drove toward downtown on this gorgeous morning.

Kaleigh found that she had the instinct to know what Hannah wanted and what she needed. Even without any real experience in caring for little ones, taking care of Hannah seemed natural. Kaleigh found herself smiling as she pushed Hannah in her stroller down the sidewalk. They walked past the toy store and Hannah noticed a colorful toy in the window. Hannah pointed and said, "Ooh," and Kaleigh couldn't resist. She picked the baby up out of the stroller, ran into the shop, and bought her the toy. The smile on Hannah's face when she handed her that special little bunny melted Kaleigh's heart.

This time, Kaleigh made it to the coffee shop before Johnathan did. It was helpful for her to be early now that she had a baby in tow. This gave her time to get Hannah settled with a bagel and cup of milk before Johnathan arrived. She taught Hannah how to suck the milk through the straw, and the two laughed back and forth as Hannah realized that the cold milk was coming into her mouth through the straw. Kaleigh enjoyed having this time to just enjoy sitting in the sunshine and take a breath. Her thoughts went to the school year and everything she had been through. It was the year her father had passed away, the year she figured out that her brother was trying to take money from her, and the year that she might have lost Jackson as a friend forever. It was also the year that she began a wonderful relationship with her cousin. All of this made the year feel incredibly long, but it was over now. There was nothing she could do about the past. She could only help to write her story for the future. There was a lot to figure out with her life. As soon as the will fiasco was over, she would begin to focus on her future. Kaleigh had always loved the idea of summer as a fresh start, a way to start again. And after the year she had, she needed it.

While Kaleigh was relaxing in the sunshine at a table outside the coffee shop, helping Hannah drink from her straw, Jackson drove by in his truck. He was on the way to make a delivery and did a double-take when he saw Kaleigh with a baby in a stroller. He pressed on the break, slowing down to get another look, not believing his eyes. He thought, "Wow, how long had he been away from her? What in the world had happened? Had Kaleigh's path truly moved away from him?" As he continued driving, his heart was a mess. He was frustrated, sad, and upset. His mind raced with, "Was that really her child? Was she with the man he had seen her with weeks before, the man in the suit? How long had it truly been since he and Kaleigh had talked?" After all these thoughts finished flooding his mind, he realized that his heart had sunk as low as it could go and that he finally had his answer. Kaleigh had moved on, and he needed to also.

When Johnathan finally arrived and found Kaleigh, he apologized multiple times for being late. Kaleigh reminded him that she was on summertime, so there was nothing to worry about. After talking about Hannah and Lola and the story behind why Kaleigh had the baby with her, Johnathan went through the details of all he had found out during his investigation. He went through the folder of artifacts he had collected and, after reviewing everything, had some papers for her to sign.

Johnathan had spoken to the staff at Havenwood as well as the doctor, and had documentation of her dad's health and his limited level of understanding and memory at the time of his trip to the lawyer's office. A copy of his last physical and memory test showed how poorly he was able to remember both short and long-term events. He had a copy of the sign-out sheet at Havenwood, showing that Wesley had taken Dad away from the property that day. The secretary at the lawyer's office was asked to provide both copies of the will and these, along with the other artifacts, would be given to the judge at the probate court, officially completing the investigation.

Kaleigh was so impressed with everything he had accomplished, leaving no stone unturned. She mentioned to him that she was nervous about the events that were yet to unfold, but Johnathan reminded her that she was not going to be alone in anything and that she didn't need to worry. Kaleigh truly appreciated that.

Once their meeting was over, Kaleigh decided to walk over to the nearby park and take Hannah to the swings before heading back home for her nap. Lola would be home by late afternoon, so Kaleigh decided afterwards that she would try her hand at making a new recipe for dinner while Hannah slept.

****

A couple of weeks went by, and Kaleigh had still not heard anything from Wesley, though Johnathan had called to let her know that her brother had decided to settle out of court. They would meet at the courthouse in a week or two, and then everything would be finalized. Johnathan figured that it would be better to meet on neutral ground and not at either lawyer's office. There would be no trial, but there would be a formal proceeding in which the judge would preside, state the facts and right the wrong. Kaleigh appreciated the fact that Johnathan had thought of everything. He had made a tough situation run as smoothly as it could. The toughest part for Kaleigh was still to come though—the rebuilding of the relationship between her and Wesley.

There were times when she was completely mad at him for what he did. It was the kind of anger where you didn't picture yourself talking to the person ever again. She was mad at him for what he did, really mad. However, there were other times that she felt sorry for him. He didn't have anyone, either. Well, who knew at this point? Maybe he had a girlfriend by now, but he didn't have any family. He was running the Garden Center, Dad's store, on his own, and over the past five years, more and more kept getting piled onto his shoulders. They never had finished their conversation about whether being in charge of everything was what he really wanted.

As the days went on, her anger subsided some and she was able to envision talking to Wesley again. Kaleigh knew that at some point, she needed to figure out when, where, and how to reach out to him. Wesley was her only sibling, and besides Lola and Hannah, he was all she had. Once the court date was behind them and a little more time had passed, Kaleigh felt more and more confident that she should reach out an olive branch and try to begin to rebuild things between them. It would be nice to get back to what they once had.

She remembered their weekly conversations and their dinners, where they connected and were able to keep up with what was happening in each other's lives. She missed that. Kaleigh didn't have much family, and she couldn't imagine life without her brother, her partner in the Garden Center, Dad's store. Plus, she was part owner of the store, so there would need to be conversations around what involvement Kaleigh would have and how she would pitch in to help. There was a lot to consider and much to figure out. But nothing could happen without being able to talk to her brother.

****

The new normal at Kaleigh's house was wonderful. Kaleigh loved coming home to laughter and company. Hannah was now crawling so fast and would pull herself up to stand whenever and wherever she could. The smile on the little one's face said, "Wow, look what I can do!" Lola and Kaleigh laughed and smiled at the little girls' proudness. Kaleigh, who did not typically take a ton of pictures, found herself being somewhat of a photographer, trying to capture these special moments. Lola seemed to appreciate the company, too, and they would talk every night after Hannah went to sleep, catching up on what was going on in each other's lives, their thoughts, their dreams.

Lola spoke more about her husband, describing him as an amazing man who was close to graduating college and along the way had worked his way up in a local company to become a manager. All while volunteering at a hospital, working toward building hours and experience toward his dream of being a school counselor. Lola had only finished one year of college and never graduated, which she figured was one reason that Ryan's parents did not approve of her. She had begun to take some education classes at the local college, but the cost was more than she could afford. The local daycare center hired her part-time, and she worked as a waitress at a pizza shop a few times per week to bring in more money. The two had gotten pregnant with Hannah before they got married. That, she figured, put his parents over the edge, and that was it—they were cut off. His parents would not answer his calls and wouldn't come to the wedding. The two decided to cancel the wedding plans and elope.

Kaleigh felt sadness for Lola. She was such a nice person and such a great mother. She didn't deserve to be cut out of her husband's family. And little Hannah might never meet her grandparents—that made her sad too. Both Lola and Kaleigh shared how grateful they were for each other. And that was when Kaleigh went through the missing pieces of her story.

She told Lola everything, all the twists and turns in her path. As she was explaining her story and looking back, she began to see so clearly and thought, "How difficult it was to see the path you are on until you can look back through the rearview mirror." She could see now, that night at Ethan and Hailey's wedding was her fork in the road. Before that night, her and Jackson's paths seemed to be winding side-by-side. Talking about the past, going through the events, helped her see that it was that night when her path began to move in a different direction from Jackson's. Between her retelling the story to Lola, and Kaleigh seeing Jackson that day in town, she realized that she truly wanted her path to come back to Jackson's.

I didn't realize at the time,
what path I was on.
I was in the dark,
But I see it now,
that my path veered away from you.
My actions, my words
pushed you away from me.
The hurt, the sadness
I feel without you in my life,
is more than I can take,
more than I can bear.
I have always wanted my path
to lead to happiness.
But it is only now
that I realize,
my path to happiness
is with you.

****

That next week, Lola shared with Kaleigh that she was excited to have been offered a job at a daycare center in the next town over. The center here did not have any openings and was small. Lola's new job was thirty-five minutes away, in a larger center and was perfect for Lola. The woman whose position she was taking was moving out of state. The job was half-time secretary and half-time teacher. And the best part was that there was room in the toddler room for Hannah. It would take a couple of weeks for the clearance paperwork and background checks to come through, but Sandra, the owner, had called to offer Lola the job.

Kaleigh was so excited for her cousin. This was just the break she needed to help her get back on her feet and begin a new life for herself and her daughter. She deserved this happy news. The two decided to celebrate with a toast. Lola was going to try the commute for a little while, but Sandra, the owner of the center, had offered her the small unattached in-law suite that was on her property. The tenant was moving out in two weeks and she had offered it to Lola and Hannah for a very small monthly rent. Lola shared how Sandra was a religious person and believed in helping people with their second chances at life. Sandra had seen something special in Lola and wanted to help her and Hannah build a new life for themselves. In tonight's conversation Lola repeated over and over how appreciative she was and how much she wanted Kaleigh to be able to get back to living her own life.

Chapter 19

For the next two weeks, Lola and Kaleigh spent time over at Danielle's house, helping her paint and prepare the nursery. They also did some shopping for Lola, Hannah, and their new place. It was fun to go shopping for a small crib that would soon change into a toddler bed for Hannah. The three tried their hand at making animal prints—some for the nursery and some for Hannah's new room. Lola was grateful to be a part of this exciting time and was even more appreciative to have friends who invited her to be a part of their circle. She hadn't felt a part of anything for a long time.

When it came time for Lola to move out, Kaleigh, Danielle, and Chris helped Lola with everything and even helped to decorate their new tiny house. It was small but cute and perfect for Lola's fresh start. Kaleigh and Danielle had some last-minute surprises to help fill the kitchen with necessities so that Lola could feel like she had everything she needed.

Lola was so thankful for everyone's help and support. Chris seemed to enjoy being with Hannah and would put her up on his shoulders as they walked down the sidewalk to get ice cream. It was fun practice for the baby girl they were expecting in winter. Danielle loved helping Lola decorate Hannah's new room and truly enjoyed the little moments when she was able to practice being a girl mom. Before they left Lola and Hannah at their new home, Kaleigh made Lola promise to keep in touch. They made a standing Saturday coffee date at the coffee shop near her new daycare center. Now that Kaleigh and Lola had found each other, Kaleigh wanted to be sure not to let their relationship fall away.

In the midst of all the busyness and the fun the girls were having was the court date. The night before, in hopes of calming some of her nerves, Kaleigh called Jeremy. They had talked a couple of times since the funeral, so Jeremy knew everything about the craziness with the will. But they had not spoken since Lola knocked on her door, so she filled him in on her new family. Jeremy was so happy that Kaleigh had her cousin to lean on through all of this. He knew what Kaleigh had gone through was a lot to deal with for anyone, but being alone would have made this difficult time so much harder.

Once Kaleigh finished talking about Hannah and Lola, Jeremy shared some news of his own. The girl that he had met through online dating turned out to be amazing. She was a nurse at the local hospital. They had finally met in person one Sunday at an Italian Restaurant for lunch, and they had been dating ever since. Kaleigh loved hearing the happiness in her friend's voice as he spoke of his Jenny. He shared how they were going to Galveston together this weekend and how excited he was to get away and spend some more time with her. When he told Kaleigh that he could see a future with her, she smiled, so happy that her best friend had found such happiness with someone. Jeremy deserved happiness as much as she did.

Then the conversation went to Jackson. Jeremy asked if anything had happened between them, and Kaleigh was sad to say no. She shared how she had sent him a letter and had gotten no reply. She mentioned seeing him a few weeks back and how she was realizing more and more the mistake she had made. When Kaleigh brought up the day she had seen him in town, the lump came back into her chest. Her heart fluttered as she replayed that day in her mind, recalling all the feelings she experienced when she saw him, a mix of sadness and excitement. Sadness that she had lost touch with such an amazing friend, and excitement to get a glimpse of him after so long.

Jeremy paused, giving some space in the conversation, space for her to think. Then he asked her the all-important question, "Do you love him, Leigh?"

Kaleigh froze at this moment and found herself unable to speak. No one had asked her that, no one had spoken that question out into the universe. Jeremy knew he had asked a big question and gave Kaleigh all the time she needed to let it sink in.

It wasn't until now, at this moment, that she realized she did love him.

After another moment of silence she quietly replied, "Yes."

Jeremy knew his friend very well, so he let her answer sink in before he continued.

"Why don't you get through the court date tomorrow and then come up with a plan? The way I see it, you have two options. One, you write him a long letter, telling him how you feel, in depth, one more time. Or two, you go and tell him in person. Your heart will tell you the way to go." Jeremy always supported Kaleigh and knew just what she needed to hear.

"What if he doesn't feel the same way anymore? What if he doesn't want me anymore?" Kaleigh almost couldn't bear the thought, but this was what scared her.

"Well, if you don't try, you will always wonder what if, and that can't be a fun place to live in." Jeremy replied in his caring tone. "Do you want to wake up every day wondering if you missed out on something special with Jackson? Wonder what could have been?"

Kaleigh let all of Jeremy's wonderful, insightful words sink in. He was right, the unknown would be so hard to live with. She wanted to know but needed to clean up the loose ends in her life first.

****

The next day, Kaleigh went on her own and met Johnathan at the courthouse an hour early. It was important to Kaleigh that she get there first and get settled, and Johnathan completely understood. He made sure to be there early as well so that she did not have to walk in alone.

Wesley got there with Dan right on time, and the judge met them all in a conference room next to the courtroom. Wesley did not say anything, and neither did Kaleigh. The lawyers did all the talking, and Johnathan did a seamless job of explaining the truths he uncovered, all the while keeping a calm tone in his voice. Even though there was some anger in Kaleigh's heart, she didn't want a fight. She didn't want any yelling or mean words exchanged. That would have made this day so much worse.

After listening to Johnathan and his report, it was the judge who had some more harsh words to say. The judge had looked everything over previously, so he knew the outcome before everyone entered the courthouse that morning. His words were strong and to the point as he said that the deceit and trickery were uncalled for. He continued, saying that this would be listed on the lawyer's record along with a hefty fine and that Wesley would be required to pay the lawyer fees for both parties. Throughout the entire speech by the judge, Kaleigh couldn't bring herself to look at Wesley. After both siblings and their lawyers signed the papers, Wesley and Kaleigh each received copies in an official envelope, and Wesley and Dan got up, without saying a word, and left the room.

Johnathan stayed with Kaleigh, and they looked over the papers in the envelope. It was a copy of the will in its previous form before the illegal last change was made, along with copies of some of the artifacts provided by Johnathan for the case. The will listed Kaleigh and Wesley as fifty-fifty owners of the Garden Center. The judge, who was very kind, let Kaleigh know that in Wesley's envelope was a copy of the fees for Johnathan's time and how and when to pay those fees. Kaleigh was very appreciative of this. Although she had always said that none of this was about the money, it did help that she did not have to pay Johnathan's bill. Kaleigh would have gladly paid him though, as he was amazing through the entire ordeal, supporting her throughout it all, more than she expected.

Leaving the courthouse, even after winning the case, all Kaleigh felt was sadness. Sadness for what had become of Wesley and her relationship. Sadness for the long road it would take to begin, to rebuild, and eventually to get back the relationship they once had. There was some worry also, as she had no idea what Wesley was feeling. Would he reach out to her? Would he be upset or angry? If he didn't reach out to her, how long should she wait to let the dust settle before she reached out to him? There were so many questions, but for now, the investigation was over, and it was time to get back to her life and her heart. She had heard the expression "Times heals all wounds," but was that really true?

Kaleigh didn't feel like going home, so she called Danielle to see if she could meet her for dinner. They decided to go to Rita's and met there at five. There was so much to say that Kaleigh felt like she was rambling on and on. Danielle was such a great friend, being there every step of the way for Kaleigh, never judging her, just listening and offering advice when needed.

Kaleigh told her about the events at the courthouse, including her nervousness, how amazing Johnathan and the judge were, and how awful she feels now about her and Wesley's relationship. The siblings had truly hit rock bottom. She shared that one minute she felt mad at her brother, and the next, she felt sadness and sorrow for him. Danielle made Kaleigh feel not crazy but instead normal, as she told her that anyone experiencing this difficult situation would feel a variety of strong emotions. The two agreed that time would be the best medicine to let the dust and the emotions of everything settle. Working with teenagers had helped both learn that when strong emotions are at the surface, no good, meaningful conversation could happen. It was when a person had calmed down and removed themselves from the situation, creating the ability to look back upon their actions, that clarity and problem-solving could occur. Kaleigh needed this validation and truly appreciated her friend's words.

Once dinner arrived, the two friends were able to change their conversation to more fun topics, such as baby names and the nursery. By dessert, they were reliving funny moments from the previous school year, and both, as always, thoroughly enjoyed each other's company. A spur-of-the-moment dinner turned out to be an amazing summer night.

CHAPTER 20

One Saturday morning in August, a week after the battle over the will was over, Kaleigh decided to finish the process of going through Mom and Dad's items in the basement. She had stopped at the store the day before to get bins to help her as she sorted keepsakes, items to sell, and things to donate.

Kaleigh spent the entire day in the basement, her mind flooded with memories, both sad and happy, and she accomplished a lot. By dinnertime, she was taking boxes to her car that would be donated to the local thrift store. There was one bin of special antiques that she wanted to take to the store in town, as it couldn't hurt to have the items checked out by a professional. She had filled and labeled four bins with treasures she had decided to keep and had found a few picture frames and trinkets to bring upstairs and put around the house. After that, she had decided to make some pasta and pour herself a glass of wine. She listened to some smooth jazz as she cooked and found it nice to relax with the thought of still more summer ahead of her. It was one more week until she would leave with Danielle for what had become their annual summer road trip. Kaleigh's goal was to finish the basement by then. Today she had gotten off to a great start.

By the time she finished dinner, it was getting dark. She was tired, maybe because of all her trips up and down the stairs, maybe it was the wine, or a combination of the two. After a long, warm shower, she decided to go to bed.

It was not long after she closed her eyes, at 10:40 p.m., that she awoke from her nightmare, as a storm rolled outside. Kaleigh took care of herself as she normally did, with a few sips of water and calm breathing. Then, as most nights when this occurred, she was able to go back to sleep.

At 12:15 a.m., it happened again. The nightmare woke her from her sleep once more. Another storm was rolling outside, with the wind seeming to be stronger this time, reigniting her nightmare. After calming herself down, she sat in bed, rubbing the back of her neck, wishing she wasn't alone.

With the therapy she had been going to, there had been one stormy night when she did not wake from a nightmare. She had thought, *Maybe the therapy is working. Maybe these horrible dreams could go away for good.* But tonight, she had no such luck. It probably didn't help that she was knee-deep in memories yesterday, going through her parents' belongings in the basement. She hadn't had more than a glass and a half of wine that night with dinner, so no trouble there.

It took her a while, tossing and turning, trying to get comfortable and clear her mind after that second nightmare, but finally, she fell back asleep. Then, at 2:45 a.m., the nightmare awoke her once more. This time, she found herself sitting upright in bed, tears rolling down her face. The storm, even louder outside now, startled her as a crack of thunder seemed to shake the entire house. She was scared, not just because of the repeating nightmare, but because she realized that she truly was alone in all of this. This past year she tried to stay so strong, to go on with her life, to try to be happy, but here she was, alone on a stormy night, crying. Would she be alone forever? Would Jackson ever forgive her? Could she find a way to get her best friend back? She so wanted to jump into his arms, as she did all those months ago on that stormy night. As these thoughts raced through her head, tears flowing down her cheeks, she realized she couldn't be alone anymore. She cared so much for Jackson. She loved him. She needed him. She couldn't take all of this on her own anymore.

Just then, another huge crack of thunder came and startled her once again. This was all too much. She couldn't take it anymore. Three minutes later, she found herself, cardigan on, keys and phone in hand, starting her car. The wind was pushing the branches of the trees around, casting back-and-forth shadows on the windshield with her back-porch light shining down. As she backed up the car to turn it around, another clap of thunder roared, and Kaleigh caught her breath. This storm just would not quit. Her heart was racing as she drove out of her driveway and turned right. No one was on the road at this hour, but there were small branches that had fallen that she tried to avoid as she drove. Her heart was racing and she could not believe that she was driving in this storm. She felt pulled to him, and at this moment, she needed to be in his arms. This storm was not going to stand in her way.

Kaleigh drove slowly, her wipers moving as fast as they could as the rain came down in buckets. The wipers would not move fast enough for as quickly as the drops were falling. The back road she took had absolutely no lights, so she was careful to take her time as she rounded the bends. She did not drive fast as there were so many branches that had fallen on the road. At one point, there was a large tree obstructing the road. She was lucky as it had fallen at an angle, giving her just enough room to veer around it and continue safely down the road.

The wind, rain, thunder and lightning continued as she drove. Kaleigh could not remember the last time a huge storm lingered on and just wouldn't quit like this one. Her heart was racing as she sat up close to the windshield, helping her to get the best view she could of the debris and the road that she could. Just before making the final turn, a bolt of lightning flashed, and she saw a huge branch of a tree come crashing down just feet in front of her! She swerved around it as she caught her breath. It was a near miss and she was incredibly lucky. At this moment, she had to remind herself to breathe.

Finally, she pulled her car into Jackson's driveway. The porch light was on, which allowed her to see that a small tree had fallen next to his driveway. She wasted no time, turning off the car, grabbing her phone and keys, and running quickly through the rain. She jumped over the trunk of the tree, stepped up on the porch, and knocked on his door. She was shaking with all the adrenalin and the stress of the drive, causing her to knock with some force, as she had so much nervous energy built up inside.

Jackson, lying awake in bed, heard three loud knocks on his door, which took him by surprise. He went to the door, looked through the window, and could not believe his eyes.

Kaleigh was standing there, drenched from head to toe. She stood there, not able to find any words at this moment. He held his hand out as if offering an olive branch, a symbol of friendship, an offer to come inside and be warm. Kaleigh grabbed his hand, and he pulled her gently inside. Before saying anything, she stood on the tips of her toes and kissed him. Not a strong pushy one, but a gentle, slow, sweet kiss. One that was deep with emotion and one that made both of their toes curl. After another moment, she pulled away from him slightly and jumped in his arms, embracing him, not wanting to let him go. He held her close, breathing in her beautiful scent, and then led her into the family room. Without saying a word, he covered her with a warm blanket, started a fire, then came to sit with her on the couch. His heart was mush. After all this time he was still a mess for Kaleigh and his feelings came back for her like a freight train barreling through the night. He had no answers, but in this moment, nothing mattered except that his Kaleigh was here, and that he loved her more then anything in this world.

The tears came back. Her crazy emotions pouring out of her. She had kept everything in and stayed strong on her own through everything that had happened this past year. And now she found herself an absolute mess. Would Jackson even still want her after all this time? What would he say? What should she say? None of these answers were ones that she had. On her drive over here, she was so focused on maneuvering through the dark branch-covered roads that she had no time to think of what she would say, what he would say.

Jackson ran his fingers through her wet hair, brushing it out of her face. Kaleigh sat up and turned to face him. He could see tears streaming down, and her rosy cheeks told him she had been crying for a while. Her heart was racing still, and all she could say was "I'm so sorry." Jackson took her face in his hands and kissed her. First, gently, softly, slowly, savoring her scent, her flavor, moving to her cheek, her neck, and then back to her soft lips. Kaleigh felt like maple syrup, weak and dripping on the floor, her heart and stomach fluttering like a family of butterflies. This, she guessed, was what love felt like, and it felt so good!

They kissed for a few minutes, and then he held her. How she had missed this, his warm strong arms around her, giving her the feeling that she was no longer alone in this scary world. She closed her eyes and took in the moment, soaked in all the feelings that were running through her, not wanting to ever forget this.

After a few moments passed, Kaleigh, leaning back against the couch, tucking her hand inside of his, looked at him and whispered, "I've been the worst friend, and I know this, but . . ." She paused, hoping she wasn't too late, and said, "I need you. I love you." She closed her eyes again, afraid for a moment of what he might say. She could feel his love for her. She knew he loved her, but what had this time apart done? Did he still want her to be his?

She felt his breathing quicken as he slowly took both hands in his. He looked deeply into her eyes and said, "I love you. I have always loved you, and I won't let you go again."

Just then, more tears streamed down her face, this time tears of joy as she realized that she wasn't too late. She didn't have to be alone anymore. He had waited for her, and she hadn't lost him as she feared. They kissed again, this time deeper and stronger than the last. Neither one of them had ever experienced this deep, true emotion with anyone before, and it was magical.

Jackson didn't want to pry tonight. He would ask her tomorrow what had happened, who the man in the suit was, about the baby, and what made her drive through a storm to get to him tonight. But until then, he was so glad she came and that she was safe. As much as he had tried to keep his distance from her, to get over her, he didn't, he couldn't. He had pretended to be over her for a long time now, but that was all it was, a lie in his head and to his heart.

After their long kiss, he got up, moved the couch and the ottoman closer to the fire, stoked the fire to make it perfect and warm, sat next to his girl, and held her close. She put her head comfortably on his shoulder, like old times, and finally felt her heart finally settle into a normal rhythm.

"Can I call you Leigh?" he asked. This question surprised her at first, but then it warmed her heart, as that was her dad's name for her. She kept her eyes closed, felt a smile come to her face, and softly replied, "Yes." They both closed their eyes as the last of the thunder rolled outside, and Kaleigh finally felt at peace. A few moments later, she was asleep.

Chapter 21

The next morning, Jackson woke first, Kaleigh still in his arms. The storm had ended, and the wind had finally stopped. The fire had gone out, and there was a chill in the air. Carefully, so as not to wake Kaleigh, he slid off the couch and walked over to the fireplace to get the fire going again. He showered, changed, and texted John, asking him to feed and check on the animals this morning and to let him know if there was any damage on the farm. He didn't want to leave Kaleigh; he didn't want her to wake up alone.

Jackson didn't even go to the diner to get breakfast. He cooked it himself. When Kaleigh finally woke up, she was confused at first and then remembered the crazy and beautiful night last night. Since the kitchen was right across from the family room, he immediately noticed her move and stretch, then turned to his coffee bar and poured her a fresh cup.

The sweet smell of a warm fire and fresh cup of coffee wafted under her nose. Being with Jackson was the perfect way to start her day. Except for her headache, things were perfect. She sat up and found herself rubbing her head above her left eye as it throbbed. Jackson leaned in for a kiss before handing her the warm cup.

"Do you need medicine?" Jackson was always so observant.

"Yes, my head is throbbing," she replied, and he went to the kitchen for medicine and a small glass of orange juice. He brought her the medicine and then returned a few minutes later with breakfast. They ate together next to the fire.

When she had almost finished her omelet, she leaned back on the couch and asked, "Do you mind if I rest my eyes a little more?" Noticing that she still looked absolutely exhausted, he brushed the hair from her face and said, "Not at all," he replied and kissed her forehead as she laid back down on the couch. He covered her with a blanket and said, "I love you."

"I love you too," Kaleigh whispered as she smiled.

While Kaleigh slept Jackson cleaned up the kitchen and went outside to check on the damage from the storm. Each time he checked on Kaleigh, she was still sleeping. It was three hours later before she woke up.

"I need a shower," she said as Jackson walked into the room. "So why don't you take one? I can freshen your clothes up in the dryer in the meantime." Jackson was happy to take care of her, to make sure she had what she needed, that she was comfortable here. He still had no idea all that she had been through.

Jackson ran to the diner while she was showering to grab some soup and sandwiches. He also decided to run into The Beverage Center to find her favorite bottle of wine and some lemon-lime soda. He knew that when her emotions were a mess, a nice cold glass of fizz could settle her stomach. He had no idea what she had been through, though the look of exhaustion in her face told him she had been through a lot.

After her shower, Kaleigh felt more like herself again. She knew that it was time to begin a deeper conversation with Jackson about all the events that led up to last night. There was so much to say, so much he didn't know. Now that she was refreshed, she felt more confident and able to handle it.

When he returned from the store, he grabbed her clothes out of the dryer and set them on the guest bed. He let her know they were there and that he would meet her on the back porch.

Kaleigh did her best to put her wet hair in a bun. Unable to brush it out, she felt this was the best option. She felt much better and appreciated her clothes being dried, soft, and warm. When she walked onto the porch, she took Jackson's breath away. She always did this to him, made him weak in the knees when she walked into a room.

Upon noticing the lunch set on the table, she said, "I don't deserve all this."

"Yes, you do," Jackson quickly replied. "You deserve all of this and more." Her smile was amazing, he thought, as he began to unwrap the sandwiches. He wasn't sure if it was too soon, but he was dying to ask, and before he knew it, out it came.

"What happened last night? I mean, I am so very glad you knocked on my door, but driving here in that horrible storm . . ." his voice trailed off, not wanting to seem too pushy, not sure if she was ready to share, not sure what her response would be.

Kaleigh took a sip of soda, a deep breath, then began. "It was a culmination of a lot of things . . ." She took another breath then shared her story, spilling out everything that had happened over the course of the past year. She told him about the horrible, terrible thing her brother had done—the deceitful switch with the will—and the hurt and pain it had caused her. As she recounted the events, Jackson felt all the hurt and pain with her. He felt awful that he had chosen to ignore her and keep his distance from her when she was going through this horrible situation. He had no idea she was going through all of this with her brother. What a jerk he must have seemed to her. She paused, taking a few bites of sandwich and soup. Then she mentioned her lawyer, Johnathan, and how amazing he was throughout the entire ordeal. At that moment, Jackson realized that the man in the suit that he saw with her that day must have been her lawyer. He would bring this up, but not now. She looked like she had so much to say and he wanted to give her space and time to do so.

Kaleigh was so hungry that she took a couple of minutes to finish her sandwich before she continued, "And my cousin, Lola, I don't know if I have ever mentioned her in our conversations. She knocked on my door one day, out of the blue. I hadn't heard from her in so long, except for sporadic text messages. She has gone through so much more than me, it makes me feel like my life isn't so bad. Her husband died last year from cancer and left a sweet baby girl without a father." She continued to tell him everything about Lola and her sweet Hannah, and how she loved taking care of her. "Oh, her smile is the sweetest thing! I can't wait for you to meet her."

Jackson's sigh was so deep that he thought for sure Kaleigh noticed. That was the last piece of the puzzle that had confused him.

Thoughts immediately ran through his head, *The baby wasn't hers; it was her cousin's.* Then Kaleigh continued, "They lived with me for a few weeks this summer. It was nice, to have a support system for a bit, and keep my mind on other things. They are my only family for now." Her voice suddenly turned sad. Jackson felt a pull on his heart with her words. He should have been there with her through everything, been her support system, but he had let her down.

Kaleigh added, "I want to make things right with Wesley, to start the conversation. I just don't know when or how. I figured I'd give him some space. But I need to come up with a plan at some point. I don't want to lose my brother forever. I mean, I am mad at him, but as the days go by more of my anger is just turning to sadness. I would like to begin to rebuild what we had. He doesn't have anyone, at least I don't think he does, I've been staying away from the store." Jackson had known that she hadn't been working at the store. But that is all that he knew.

While Kaleigh sipped on her soup and looked out over the beautiful farm, Jackson couldn't keep his eyes off of her. As she looked back toward him, he reached out for her hand. She put her hand inside his and he gave it a squeeze. The peacefulness of the farm and Jackson's company were just what she needed right now.

There was just so much to say, so she continued, "Oh, and I took your advice. I have been going to a therapist in Colby. She is great, helping me work through everything I have been through. Thank you for suggesting it." She paused to take a breath of fresh air. "I have had one stormy night so far without waking up with the nightmare, so I know I am making progress."

"That's good." He was happy with the progress she was making and happy she had taken his advice. He didn't know if he should tell her that last night he didn't sleep at all because he was so worried about her. With every clap of thunder, gust of wind and bolt of lightning, he worried how Kaleigh was doing. Part of him wanted to go to her last night as the storms continued to rage outside, but he froze and couldn't bring himself to do it.

Kaleigh stood at this moment, stretched a bit, and slowly walked over to the railing, looking out over the farm. She sighed and then continued her story. "Then came yesterday. It was an emotional day, but I felt good in the moment. Lola and Hannah moved out recently and yesterday I decided to work in the basement, to go through what was left of Mom and Dad's things. The memories were sweet, revisiting the past as I chose what to keep and what to let go of. I finally felt ready to do it. I mean, it was emotional, and tiring, but it felt good. I worked all day but managed to make myself dinner, had a little bit of wine, and went to bed. It wasn't very late when I crawled turned out the light. I was exhausted," she added, still feeling tired after all she had been through.

Jackson stayed quiet and just took in all that Kaleigh was saying. At this moment she took a break from speaking and just took in the beauty of the farm. Her heart was calm, her headache had subsided and she was relaxed.

"So what happened?" Jackson asked as he got up, walking over to her. "Last night, when the storms kept coming, the nightmares wouldn't stop. After waking up a second time I had trouble falling back to sleep. I had a few tears fall as I thought back to the time you were there with me, that night you stayed with me." Jackson had remembered back to that night quite a bit in these past few months. He never forgot how scared he felt for her, and knew that if he had not been there, he may never have known of her nightmares.

Kaleigh turned to Jackson at this moment, taking his hands in hers, "And by the third time the storm woke me up I just cried, I couldn't take it anymore. The thunder cracked so loudly. I was scared, alone, and falling apart. It was the worst feeling, and suddenly I found myself being pulled to you, needing you. The next thing I knew, I was driving through the heavy rain, veering past branches that had fallen in the road, and then here I was, knocking on your door."

At this moment, Jackson took her face in his hands, looked into her eyes and said, "I'm so sorry I wasn't there for you through everything. I realize now that I let you down . . . I should have been there" She looked into his eyes and said, "I'm sorry it took me so long to realize that you are the one for me, that you are my person." She paused just for a second, then said, "The one I love." And with those words, he kissed her, slow and deep, his heart racing with happiness as the butterflies returned. He had never fallen out of love with Kaleigh. In fat it was the exact opposite. The feelings he had now told him that in this time apart from her, his love for her had only grown.

Jackson never wanted to be apart from Kaleigh again. This strong, beautiful woman had been through so much, and he had let her down, had walked away from her, and as they kissed, he vowed to himself never to let her go again.

He pulled away from her lips, took a deep breath, and found himself repeating his words, "I'm so sorry I wasn't there for you, Leigh." He kissed her again and led her to the couch on the other side of the porch. He knew that he needed to explain his side of the story, the confusion, the jealousy. He knew it would be difficult, but she had opened her heart to him and now it was his turn.

As they sat down, he stroked his hands through her hair, kissed her once more, then began, "That night that I was supposed to take you to dinner, the week your father passed, I came to pick you up, and his car was there. I didn't know who it was at the time but figured out later it was Jeremy. The jealousy came hard Kaleigh. I was upset. My heart felt stiff, like a rock inside my chest. That entire week was so difficult for me. I wanted to be the one who was there for you, holding your hand, walking with you on the day of the funeral. I know you said there wasn't anything romantic between you two, but it still hurt." Jackson paused, and Kaleigh didn't say a word as she felt a lump in her chest, knowing she had made a big mistake.

"And then he called you Leigh, and I almost lost it. I had never heard anyone call you by that name before, except your dad. It seemed like a privilege to call you that, and I was so hurt. I was a fool, and I'm sorry. I let my feelings get the best of me. In all of that jealousy I decided that I had better keep my distance, try to let you go, that maybe we weren't meant to be. It hurt so bad, but I knew I had to try. I kept my distance because seeing you would just bring back the hurt. It was too hard for me to see you, knowing you weren't going to be mine."

That was a lot for Kaleigh to take in at this moment, but Danielle had been right. It was jealousy that had taken him away from her. He paused to give her another kiss, a soft one, then continued.

"I want you to know you never left my mind, I tried to take my mind move elsewhere, to think of other things, but it was no use. I thought about you every day. Then I got your letter, and I wanted to come and see you, but it never seemed to work out." He looked away for a moment, trying to find the courage to continue with what he now knew were big misunderstandings on his part. "I saw you at the coffee shop twice—once with a man, who I assume now was your lawyer, and once with the baby. Oh man, that day I saw you with the baby, I was so confused, wondering how truly long it had been since we last saw each other. Was I going crazy? Had you really had a baby? I was starting to lose my mind. In that moment I thought the worst, that we were truly through, but even then I couldn't get you out of my mind."

While he was pouring his heart out to her, he held both of her hands as he looked into her eyes. He kissed her again, then continued, "I shouldn't have tried to let you go. I should have come and talked to you. I shouldn't have let jealousy keep me from you. Then you wouldn't have been alone, Leigh. I'm so sorry."

"No, It's my fault," Kaleigh couldn't let him take all of the blame. "I should have come to talk to you. I'm the one who said I didn't feel the same way, the night of the wedding. It was me who pushed you away. And I should have been more conscious of my time the week of the funeral." Kaleigh paused at this moment, feeling the weight of Jackson's guilt and frustration with himself, not wanting him to carry all the weight of this.

A tear came again to her cheek, and he wiped it away as she continued, "I know I don't deserve you, Jackson, but I need you in my life, every day… if you'll have me. I can't do this alone."

At that moment, Jackson took her face in his hands once more and said, "You are not to solely to blame, Leigh. It was my fault too, but you don't have to be alone anymore. You'll never lose me again," and kissed her, at first soft and slow, then long and deep. The butterflies in her stomach and tingles all over returned with the long, sensual kiss. In the middle of the kiss, he pulled gently away and said, "I promise, I'll never let you go."

Kaleigh realized in that moment that he was everything she needed, and that this moment, months in the making, was meant to be. It was genuine. It was perfect. It was love. She felt relieved, she felt strong again, and she was. . . home.

Chapter 22

Kaleigh's exhaustion had gotten the best of her. Waking up every day and pushing through the stresses of life, and all the challenges of the past school year, trying to stay strong, everything had now come crashing down on her. As she recounted the stories, her emotions had come spilling out of her, leaving her body, and her mind, exhausted.

They held each other, they kissed, and she slept. She stayed at Jackson's house and, for hours at a time, she slept, finding comfort in different places. Sometimes she laid on the couch on the back porch. Other times she napped by the fireplace. And overnight, she slept next to him in his bed. Jackson found himself staring at her while she slept and, at times he stroked her hair, as if to make sure that what was happening was real. For so long he had lost all hope and now, everything he had dreamed of was coming true. Jackson didn't want to push things too fast, so there was no love making that weekend. Instead they touched, they held each other, and it felt amazing.

****

When Kaleigh finally returned home, she noticed the aftermath of the recent storms in her own yard and realized she had some cleaning up to do. She did her best to pick up as many branches and sticks as she could over the period of about an hour and put them in cans at the end of her driveway. Then she took a long, hot shower and called her best friend, Danielle.

"Oh my gosh, Kaleigh, I have tried to call you so many times, but your phone was off." Danielle said in a worried voice.

"I'm sorry, my phone died. I spent the weekend—" she paused— "at Jackson's!" Kaleigh couldn't keep the excitement from her voice.

"What? Are you serious?" Danielle's worried voice turned to that of happiness very quickly.

"Yes, oh, Danielle, we figured out everything. It turns out Jackson had seen me a few times in town, once with Johnathan and another with Hannah, and you were right, he was completely jealous of Jeremy. All that had made him upset and confused, and made him believe that I had moved on. We talked all weekend, held each other, and kissed. Oh, his kiss, it is amazing, like nothing I have ever felt!"

"Oh, Kaleigh, I am so excited for you! How did all of this happen?" Danielle asked. Then she added, "I tried to call you Saturday morning and then again last night to make sure you were OK after all the storms. I was getting so worried."

"I'm sorry I worried you. The night of the storms, I woke up three times with my nightmare, and by the last time I was just bawling. I was so scared, and felt more alone than I had ever felt in my entire life. I realized I couldn't, I didn't want to be alone anymore. The tears wouldn't stop and the next thing I knew, I was driving in the heavy rain, dodging branches in the road, driving to him."

"Oh gosh, you drove in that storm?" Danielle interrupted.

"Yes, I couldn't believe it either. It was like I was being pulled to him, like something out of a movie, running through the rain, knocking on his door, not knowing what he would say." She paused for a moment. "But he was so happy that I came. We sorted everything out, and the weekend was amazing! He took care of me and we talked about everything, his story and mine, and I slept, a lot. It was like reliving everything that had happened these past few months just took away all of my energy. Jackson was amazing. He listened, he cooked for me, he held me . . . " a huge smile came to Kaleigh's face as she recalled the past couple of days. "Oh, Danielle, I finally felt the butterflies, and . . . I told him I love him!"

"Kaleigh, that is amazing! I'm so happy for you." Danielle was truly happy for her friend, "So it was jealousy and misunderstandings that kept him from coming to see you?"."

"Yes, Jackson was going to come and see me, he tried to, but had ended up in heartbreak and confusion when he saw me with Johnathan and then with Hannah. In looking back at the months of not seeing him, now I understand everything. I finally had my questions answered. I know that he feels terrible, that he wasn't with me through everything with Wesley, and blames himself for everything. I couldn't let him take all of the blame though. I told him it was my fault for pushing him away."

"I am so happy that you both figured things out, and that you have each other. That is what I have always wished for Kaleigh, for you and Jackson to figure things out, to realize that you were meant for each other!" Danielle could not contain her excitement and you could hear it in her voice as she spoke, so incredibly happy for her friend.

The two continued talking for another half an hour. They talked about how Danielle was feeling, and Kaleigh asked if she was ready for the trip the two were going to take this weekend. Danielle shared that she was in bed with some huge pain from her sciatic nerve and that there were times she couldn't even stand up straight. The baby was pinching a nerve and was making it rough for her this weekend. As Danielle was sharing this, she had an idea.

"Oh, Kaleigh, I think that you should take Jackson on our weekend away! Wouldn't it be so wonderful for you two to start your life together with a weekend away?" Danielle hadn't thought of this idea until just now and was so excited!

"But it is our weekend, Danielle. Our tradition." Kaleigh was a little sad, but Danielle quickly interrupted, "I know, but I don't think this pain is going to go away quickly from what the doctor says. And I won't be any fun if this pain is still here. Walking is tricky for me, and you are not pushing me around in a wheelchair! And besides, you and Jackson need a special time in a special place to be together. You both deserve it. Please tell me you will ask him to go. You and I can plan something together another time. We can always take the baby next year or leave her with Chris. I promise we will go away again." Danielle knew that she was rambling on, but really hoped that her friend would take her up on the offer.

After thinking about it for a moment, Kaleigh asked, "Are you sure? This would be our last getaway before the baby comes."

"Yes, I'm sure. I promise we will go again next year." Danielle meant every word she said, even though it made her slightly sad that she wasn't going. She was so happy thinking about the exciting vacation that her best friend could share with her new love.

"OK," Kaleigh said with excitement in her voice, "I would love to go away with him. I will ask him."

"Yes!" Danielle replied, unable to contain her excitement. Before hanging up, Kaleigh promised to come and see her tomorrow.

****

Jackson did not hesitate to say yes when Kaleigh asked him to come on vacation with her. He quickly made arrangements so that he could go. Kaleigh was shocked that he said yes so quickly. There were only a few days to finish her work in the basement and get ready for the trip, and she was able to finish the task.

She was both nervous and excited about their time together. It was the same beach town that she and Danielle had gone to last year, one with on-and-off-the-beaten-path great places. One where you would probably find things this year that you didn't know existed the last time you were there. Plus, it would be exciting to show Jackson around, to spend some quality time with him, and extremely special to have her first couple of romantic nights with him.

Kaleigh had purchased a silk nightgown—nothing fancy or showy, just long and beautiful. She had also gotten her nails done and put a few curls in her hair before she put the last few things in her bag. Jackson was picking her up, and she made sure that she had everything she needed, but that she didn't pack too much, and that she looked nice but not overdone.

When Jackson saw her at the door, he couldn't speak and found himself stumbling over his words. "You're . . . you look beautiful!"

"Thank you!" Kaleigh replied as he took her bags and then held her hand as she locked the door and they walked to the truck. The conversation on the way to the beach town was amazing. The two laughed, shared more about their families, and talked so much about food that they found themselves stopping at a Food Truck Rodeo that they had seen a sign for. They bought food from three different trucks and thoroughly enjoyed themselves as they tried the variety of choices.

While driving, Jackson couldn't stop holding her hand. He was nervous and excited about their weekend away, and ever since Kaleigh had called to invite him on her weekend getaway, he had imagined what being with her would be like. The excitement was growing by the minute, and he felt happier in this moment than he had ever felt in his entire life.

That night at the hotel, after changing and freshening up in the bathroom, Kaleigh came into the room. Jackson watched as Kaleigh walked toward him in her lavender nightgown. It was long and flowing, just like her hair. It didn't show too much, but wow, he was speechless. She was perfect, not just in this moment but always. He stood up and walked toward her, meeting her halfway. He took her in his arms and took in her scent. As if there were a slow song playing in the background, he held her and rocked back and forth with her in a slow dance. It was an unexpected, beautiful moment between the two, and Kaleigh found herself placing her head on his shoulder and closing her eyes. She wanted to remember this moment forever.

The next hour was spent in slow motion, or so it seemed. They explored each other and took everything moment by moment so as to savor and remember every touch, every feeling. Like waves on an ocean, emotion and love ebbed and flowed between the two. The only words that were said were from Jackson: "I've been waiting for this night." Jackson was so gentle with her, taking great care to show how much he loved her without being overpowering or rushed. And for Kaleigh, the night was so much better than she could have ever imagined. The night was perfect. And, waking up in his arms the next morning was everything she needed and more. They both found it difficult to get out of bed as they continued to explore and excite each other. The feelings they shared were that of dreams, but it wasn't a dream, it was real and it was wonderful!

Kaleigh loved seeing Jackson so relaxed this weekend. And Jackson loved seeing Kaleigh so happy. The two had a perfect weekend together—perfect weather, perfect company, and just the right mix of love and tourist activities. They only separated for a few minutes when Kaleigh decided to go into a second clothing store, and Jackson had his eye on something at a jewelry store. He didn't tell her he was slipping into the store, just that he would meet her at the ice cream shop in twenty minutes. Jackson had found something just perfect for Kaleigh, though he wasn't planning on giving it to her quite yet.

Kaleigh did not want to talk about serious topics until the way back home. The two had made a pact and stuck to the plan. She wanted this mini-vacation to be relaxing, not stressful. She wanted to keep things light and to work to get to know Jackson even more. During their getaway the two never had to work at the conversation, it came easy, just as it always had between the two. Jackson had always felt like he could talk to Kaleigh forever without even having to try hard, and Kaleigh felt the same way.

It wasn't until on the way home when Kaleigh finally brought up Wesley, wanting his opinion on what she should do.

"I know we said we wanted to have a relaxing vacation, but now that we are almost back home, can you help me figure out what to do about Wes?" Kaleigh always appreciated Jackson's opinion and had missed being able to talk to him, confide in him, and get his opinion on things these past few months.

"What do you want to know?" Jackson wanted a little clarification before he added his two cents.

"Well, first, have you seen him? How does he seem?" Kaleigh hadn't stepped foot into the store in so long and had only seen him that one day at the courthouse last month.

Jackson waited a moment, then replied, "I have seen him a couple of times, and, you know, he seems normal. I mean, he still walks around with his clipboard, running his fingers through his hair on occasion, directing traffic and employees with a pretty good attitude. It's mostly the same staff there, with a couple of new ones. I mean, I couldn't tell there was anything going on. He has seemed normal this entire time." Kaleigh really trusted Jackson's words more than he probably knew.

"I'm just worried about what will happen when I walk in one day." Kaleigh imagined it going three ways. "I mean, will he avoid me and not speak to me? Will he pretend like nothing happened? Or will he wait until we get to the back room and start yelling?"

"That's a tough one, but either way, I don't think you should go see him for the first time alone." Kaleigh thought for a moment and realized that Jackson had a great point. "I mean, I don't see him making a big scene at the store, but you never know. If someone is with you, I think you will have more luck in keeping him calm. Though my thought is, I don't think the first time you see him should be at the store. I think you should meet on neutral ground." As Kaleigh let his ideas sink in, she realized that Jackson's words made perfect sense.

"Yeah, but he probably doesn't want to see me. I don't even know if I am ready to see him either. There are days I still wake up extremely mad at him. But I am trying to be the better person and move past this. I am half-owner of the store, so I know that I need to figure out my new place there, how I will step up and help. I keep thinking that maybe I need to begin working again before the pumpkin patch rush, but that means we'd have to be talking before then." Kaleigh made some great points, Jackson thought, as she spoke in a completely caring voice. She was handling this so much better than he would. He was proud of her for wanting to forgive Wesley and move past this so soon. If the tables were turned, he didn't think that Wes would be ready to forgive so quickly.

"I am so proud of you for wanting to push past the hurt so quickly. I don't know if I could. I mean, if it was me dealing with that. But whatever happens, whatever you decide, I will be here for you. If you want me to help you, to be with you when you speak to him, I absolutely will be. If you want me to stay back and let you handle it, that's OK too." Jackson reached over at this moment and squeezed her hand. It was as if his gesture was saying, "I'm not going anywhere." and Kaleigh appreciated that so very much. She felt better now that she got her feelings off her chest, and that she had Jackson to help her navigate this next step. She just had to figure out what that step would be and when she felt ready to move ahead. She hoped that she would know in her heart when it was time.

****

When Jackson dropped Kaleigh off at home, he asked her if she wanted him to stay the night. He would have to leave early in the morning to get back to work, but he wasn't ready to say goodbye to her yet. Kaleigh was excited to have Jackson with her longer. It wasn't until now that she realized that they would need to figure out their new normal, especially with the school year ahead.

Just as they were about to sit down to dinner, the phone rang. Kaleigh glanced at the phone and noticed Jeremy's name on the screen. "Is it OK if I take this call quick? I haven't had a chance to tell Jeremy about us yet. He will be so happy! He kept telling me that I needed to find you, to tell you how I felt." Jackson replied, "No, not at all," then a smile came to his face as he thought, *Hey, this Jeremy isn't such a bad guy after all!*

Kaleigh was so excited to share the news with her friend as she put the phone on speaker. She let him know that Jackson was there and the two said hello. "I finally went to Jackson and told him everything!" Kaleigh said in such an excited and happy voice. The memory of that weekend still fresh in her mind. Jeremy immediately asked when this all happened and Kaleigh told him quickly of her crazy idea to drive to him in a horrible storm last weekend.

"Sounds pretty romantic to me, but that's not one of the ideas I gave you!" Jeremy replied.

Kaleigh laughed. "I know, but so worth it," she answered to Jeremy as she gave Jackson a quick wink.

"Congratulations, you two! Jackson, hey, how's it going?" Jeremy was really turning out to be a nice guy in Jackson's eyes.

"Thanks, and much better now. This girl really threw me for a loop—well, a couple of them, actually." Jackson shared with Jeremy the confusion he felt upon seeing Kaleigh in town twice: first with the lawyer and then with a baby. He shared that, in looking back, it was something to laugh about now, but living through it was a punch to the gut, the worst months of his life.

Jeremy agreed with Jackson, saying, "Well, you do appreciate things more when you have had to climb to get to them." Jackson couldn't agree more. He quietly walked behind Kaleigh, hugged her from behind and began to kiss her neck. Kaleigh turned around, gave him a sweet kiss and Jackson continued to hold her as they talked.

"Hey, I won't keep you two, but I wanted to share some news!" Jeremy continued.

"Ooh, I'm intrigued!" Kaleigh said with a happy laugh.

"What are you guys doing on Christmas Eve?" asked an excited Jeremy on the other end of the line.

"Wow, not sure we have talked about Labor Day yet, let alone Thanksgiving or Christmas. Why?" Kaleigh said with a playful voice.

"Jenny and I are getting married, and you two have to come!"

There was a slight pause as Kaleigh let the news sink in. Then she replied, "Oh gosh, are you serious?" She paused to look at Jackson and smile. "That is wonderful, Jeremy!"

As Kaleigh shared her excitement, she made a thumbs-up signal to Jackson as if to ask, "Are you on board with this?" without saying it out loud. Jackson gave a thumbs-up signal in return, and Kaleigh shared that they would definitely be there. "Texas, here we come!" Kaleigh replied, and soon after, they ended the call. She was so excited for Jeremy and could not wait to meet Jenny. This would make for a fun holiday season!

That night, as he held Kaleigh, Jackson realized he had too many words swirling in his head that would not leave him, would not allow him to relax. He was still extremely upset with himself for leaving Kaleigh alone for all those months, and he felt like if he kept everything inside, he would burst. They had talked about the events that unfolded, but Jackson wanted to make sure she knew that he would never let it happen again.

"I am so sorry for not being there for you all those months." He whispered as he caressed her arm. Kaleigh had closed her eyes but was awake and relaxed.

"We've talked about this, remember it was both of our faults, we were both to blame." Kaleigh's voice was calm, quiet, meaningful.

"I know," Jackson continued, "but I don't know if I can ever forgive myself for letting you down, leaving you hanging, wondering what happened as you were carrying so much on your shoulders. I am so incredibly sorry and I hope you can forgive me"

"Jackson . . ." Kaleigh began to say something but Jackson quietly put his finger on her lips and whispered, "Hold on, just let me say this." Then he turned on his side, lifted himself up and turned so he could look into her eyes. "I want you to know, that whatever comes your way, I will be here for you. I promise I will never leave you, even if something happens to make me jealous – I promise to talk to you. Nothing will stand in my way from helping you, from being there." And at this moment, as he stared deep in her eyes and reached up to brush the hair from her face, "Whatever help you need, whether it's holding your hand and walking next to you, or standing right behind you as you take the lead, I will help you, support you, love you . . . forever." As she heard those words she put her hands to his face, pulled him to her and kissed him, slow and long. She paused the kiss long enough to whisper, "Thank you, my love," then kissed him again. Kaleigh's heart had melted and she realized that she had become the luckiest girl in the world.

Chapter 23

Most Saturday mornings Kaleigh was able to drive over to see Lola and Hannah near their new home. She cherished these moments as time spent getting to know her new extended family. Continuing the connection between them was important, and, besides her time with Jackson, was the highlight of her week. It was at the coffee shop one Saturday morning where Hannah took her first steps, and where Kaleigh shed a tear of happiness that she was able to witness the milestone. Kaleigh and Lola both played the proud mom as they took videos of the moment on their phones.

Lola shared how much she loved her job, and how Hannah loved her teachers and friends in the toddler room. Sandra continued to be a support to the two, inviting them over for dinner once per week, and was always looking for ways to help them, finding anything they needed. Lola felt lucky, special, and blessed. After all she had been through, Kaleigh could not think of a better person for these blessings to happen to.

Hannah's birthday was right around the corner and one Saturday after coffee, the three walked to the ice cream shop to find out about having a small party for Hannah there. It was the perfect spot to celebrate a one-year-old and the theme would be llamas, the little one's new favorite animal! Kaleigh paid the deposit and ordered the decorations, and when Lola questioned her generosity she simply said, it's for my new family. Kaleigh felt blessed to have Lola and

Hannah drop on her doorstep a few months before and was excited to help create this special memory.

In a more serious conversation one Saturday, Lola told her how she really felt like her life was coming back together after it felt broken for so long. She shared how she had felt stuck, not able to figure out what to do, almost feeling frozen. Kaleigh could relate to the feeling of brokenness and shared how fallen apart she felt that night of the storms, like her life was broken, that she was more alone than she had ever felt. She spoke of how, even though she hadn't lost someone as Lola did, the fact that she was all alone without Jackson was more than she could take. The drive through the storm changed her path for the better. And the beautiful weekend they shared and the trip to the coast would be memories she would never forget. Lola was so happy that Kaleigh had finally found her happiness. The two embraced in a hug and tried to avoid the tears. The cousins were so grateful to have each other, and relieved that they had each found the path they were meant to be on, their path to happiness.

As they left the coffee shop that day, Kaleigh had a spur of the moment idea to take some family photos of the two near the pretty flowers that lined the sidewalk. A passerby was even able to take a nice picture of the three of them. Before Kaleigh said goodbye, she thought to ask Lola if she had a few pictures she could have of Hannah as she grew over the past year and a picture of her father. Lola agreed to send her some photos this afternoon while Hannah was napping. Kaleigh did not share the plan with her cousin but knew these photos would make for a perfect gift!

****

Jackson had been so busy since the two returned from their weekend away that he wasn't able to meet Lola and Hannah before the birthday party. It was Labor Day Weekend and time to celebrate the precious little girl. Chris, Danielle, and Jackson came to the party, as well as a couple of Lola's new friends from the daycare. Sandra was there, and Kaleigh was able to thank her for giving Lola a second chance and for being such a support to her cousin. The party was perfect in every way. And by the end of the party, Kaleigh found a quiet moment to give Lola the photo book she had created of Hannah's first year of life. Lola fought back the tears as she turned the pages and then gave Kaleigh the biggest hug for this generous gift. Sandra flipped through the pages afterward and learned more about Lola's story. It made her happy to be a part of Lola's new chapter in life. Sandra had always prided herself in being a good judge of character, and she realized that her instincts paid off once again in the hiring and helping of Lola.

Perhaps the most surprising thing about the day was Jackson. Kaleigh had never seen Jackson with any young child before, but he was drawn to Hannah and her to him. The entire party Hannah walked back and forth from the Chris to Jackson. Jackson would make a funny face at her to get her to laugh, and she would let out a squeal and head back to see Chris. In between bites of ice cream, she would waddle back to Jackson for hugs, and at one point, she sat on his lap, playing with one of her new toys. While Lola, Kaleigh, and Danielle sat and talked, they couldn't help but smile at Hannah and her new friend. At one point, Chris and Jackson took turns making their respective stuffed animals give Hannah a hug and a kiss, causing the little one to laugh in such giddiness! Kaleigh found herself feeling even more affection toward Jackson upon seeing him in this new element. She didn't think her love for Jackson could deepen any further until today, when it did.

As the school year began to get underway, Kaleigh helped Danielle make sure that the nursery was ready and the house was set to welcome a little one. Kaleigh worked with the secretaries in the main office to plan a baby shower for Danielle, and they decided to make it a surprise in early October. There was a secret box in the office where staff members could pick a diaper pin that had a needed gift written on it to help make sure Danielle got all the finishing touches on her wish list.

Kaleigh and Jackson figured out their new normal. On school nights, Kaleigh would sleep at her place, and on weekends, she would go to Jackson's. They ate together many nights but had a couple to themselves as well so that they could keep up with their jobs. And whenever the street fair came back, they made sure to go, eating such great food, enjoying each other's company, holding hands, and walking beneath the twinkling lights like they did so long ago as friends. It was such a sentimental place as they both felt like this was where their story began so long ago.

The week before Danielle's baby shower, Kaleigh decided that she was ready to have a conversation with Wesley. Jackson suggested inviting Wesley to dinner with the two of them. He would deliver the produce that Friday, tell Wesley about his new relationship with Kaleigh, and invite him to dinner. The ball would be in Wesley's court, and he would choose whether or not to show up. If he came, the restaurant would be neutral ground, and the end result might go better. Kaleigh liked the idea and thought it was definitely worth a shot.

Jackson began Operation Reconciliation by walking up to Wesley after the produce was set for the day. He started the conversation with some small talk about the weather and how things were going at the store. Then he began to go deeper into the conversation.

"Hey, I don't know if you've heard but, Kaleigh and I are together now." Jackson wasn't sure what he'd say, but he had to tell him.

Wesley paused for a moment, "Wow, that's cool" was all he could muster.

Then, Jackson went for it, "Hey, Kaleigh and I would love for you to meet us for dinner this weekend. Are you free?" There were crickets, and for quite a few moments, nothing was said. Crickets. Jackson had no idea what was going through Wesley's mind, what he would say but waited patiently for a response.

Finally, in true Wesley fashion, he ran his hand through his hair and said, "Maybe, I have to check my schedule."

Jackson replied, "OK, we will be at Rita's tomorrow night at seven. Kaleigh would love to see you." He was careful to make sure Wesley knew that Kaleigh was on board with the dinner.

Wesley stayed silent for a few moments, then finally said, "OK, See ya later," and walked away. It seemed to Jackson that he had caught Wesley off-guard. Wesley, in his own way, seemed to stay calm, as if nothing bothered him, when deep down, maybe he was squirming, or nervous. Jackson couldn't pin-point any emotion from Wesley through their short conversation. But Jackson wasn't anxious at all and felt accomplished that he had done what he said he would, start the process toward rebuilding a broken relationship. He knew that Kaleigh would be anxious and nervous and he was determined to be there for her, whenever and whatever she needed. Only time would tell what happened next.

****

The night that Wesley was invited to meet Jackson and Kaleigh at Rita's was a rainy one. The two arrived early and sat at a quiet corner table. As Kaleigh sipped on her drink she kept the conversation with Jackson going as she was determined not to stare at the door to the restaurant or at her phone. She wanted to be relaxed and keep her emotions calm. Jackson being there kept her calm. It was the unknown that made her nervous. Kaleigh was sure that if Wesley came she would settle a bit, knowing that he was ready to talk. If Welsey didn't come, she had a feeling that her emotions would elevate. It was the not knowing that made her truly nervous.

As it turned out, Wesley did not come. When Kaleigh finally looked at her phone to check the time and saw 7:14 p.m., she knew that her brother wasn't going to show. She decided to take a breath and try to enjoy the evening, but it was hard. She was mad at Wesley for not meeting her halfway. He had been the one to make a mess of things, not her. *Was he not sorry? Did he not have any empathy? Did Wesley not have any desire to make things better between them?* These were all questions swimming through her head and making her heart race. Jackson could see the worried look in her eyes and knew that Kaleigh's mind was racing. He set his drink down, placed a hand on hers and whispered, "Don't be upset, we will keep trying." It was these words that made her brain settle and her heart melt all at once. Jackson was her calming force, and he was right. There wasn't anything she could do in the moment except relax and enjoy each others' company. They couldn't change the fact that Wesley did not walk through that door. They would not give up, but allow time and space to help in the healing.

"I'm just disappointed is all. I know being or staying mad won't change anything. Maybe he does need more time and space. And if that's what he wants, that is what I'll give him . . . I don't know what I would do without you Jackson?"

Then he said, "We will give him some time, and then, maybe we need to come at this from a different angle. Maybe he needs to hear from you before we get him to come for dinner. I thought maybe the dinner would be a nice neutral place to meet, but he must not be ready for that."

"You are so wise!" Kaleigh said with a smile, then she squeezed his hand and leaned over to give him a kiss. She really was the luckiest girl. "Thanks for helping me stay strong through all of this," she added.

"You are stronger than you realize Kaleigh Evans," Jackson replied then leaned in until his lips met hers in a soft kiss. When the warm soft kiss was over, she fell into his arms and he held her.

****

The afternoon of the baby shower, Danielle was paged to the library as soon as the buses had pulled away. As she heard her name over the speaker she peered into the hallway and realized how eerily quiet it seemed. Her tiredness kept her from thinking that a baby shower could be the reason. Instead, she wondered what book the librarian was looking for.

As soon as Danielle walked in, twenty staff members and her husband yelled, "Surprise!" as pink balloons fell from the ceiling. The mom-to-be caught her breath, put her hands to her face and smiled. She walked toward Chris, who met her halfway, and they embraced in a hug. Then her eyes met Kaleigh's and she mouthed the words, "Thank you!" Danielle was extremely surprised and very grateful that so many people had gone to all of this trouble for her.

Chris knew about everything and was happy to be a part of this special event. It was fun to see what gifts they received and to hear everyone's advice for the new parents. Kaleigh had made some delicious treats, part of her baking experiment, which was turning out very well. It appeared that Kaleigh had gotten much of her mom's baking talent, and she loved doing it. The afternoon was very special, and Kaleigh, after cleaning up the library, ended up at Danielle's house afterwards and the friends talked for an hour around the kitchen table. The gifts were amazing and Danielle finally felt ready for the baby to arrive. She was due just after Thanksgiving, but they knew the baby would come when she was ready. Kaleigh was so excited for her friend to have everything she needed and to finally be growing her little family.

Chapter 24

A couple of weeks passed by and Kaleigh realized she had to reach out again to Wesley. Jackson was probably right. Wesley deserved to hear from her before he was thrown into a dinner with company. One Saturday, she took a break from her lesson plans and grading and wrote her brother a letter.

My brother,

I have missed you. I want to talk to you, to make things right, and to figure out my place in the business. I can't imagine how difficult things have been for you suddenly having everything on your shoulders.

You are my only family and I don't want to lose you. I realize things may be awkward with everything that has happened but I want to talk. I want to figure things out. I want to help you. I miss my brother and I want you back in my life.

Can we talk? Please text or call when you can.

Love,

Kaleigh

Kaleigh worked the rest of the morning on her work for school. Then she decided to take a shower and drop off the note to Wesley at the Garden Center. She wasn't sure if she would hand the note to him directly or place it on his desk, so she sealed it in a lavender envelope. Kaleigh had taken the time to write his name and draw a flower on the outside of the envelope to show some care and make it stand out in case she ended up leaving it on his desk.

By the time she walked into the store, it was late afternoon. The place was busy with families choosing the perfect pumpkin. She walked slowly through the aisles inside the store, noticing how great everything looked. Two staff members who had been there for years came up to give Kaleigh a hug and ask her how she was doing. They talked for a few minutes, and then Kaleigh made her way to the back office. Peeking inside before actually stepping foot in, she did not see anyone. As she walked to Dad's old desk, she noticed that all of the photos were still there, untouched—a photo of Mom, one of the family, one of Dad and Wesley outside the store, and one of Kaleigh and Dad in the flower fields.

Then, out of the corner of her eye, she saw a new frame, and in it was a picture of Wesley with his arm around a girl she didn't recognize. Wow, if Wesley had found someone, that would be wonderful, Kaleigh thought. Even after what he had done, she wanted him to be happy. She felt ready to forgive him and move on. Absolutely, she wanted her brother to have the same kind of happiness that she had found in Jackson. Pausing for another moment, she took one more look at the photo, left the letter standing up in front of the computer, and left. On her way out of the store she looked for Wesley but didn't see him.

At dinner that night, she told Jackson about the letter and what she had seen in the office at the Garden Center. She told him how the office was mostly unchanged from how Dad had left it, which made Kaleigh happy. She also shared of the photo of Wesley with a girl she did not know. And that, for some reason, that photo had given Kaleigh hope.

****

The weeks that followed seemed to move along very fast. At times it was difficult to keep up with all her schoolwork, and there were many nights she brought her computer to Jackson's to have a working dinner. Those types of dinners were ones where bites of food were mixed in with typing on the computer, entering grades, finishing lesson plans and replying to emails. On these nights Jackson was amazing and got Kaleigh everything she needed so that she could keep working. One night after the meal, he made her a hot chocolate, then came up behind her, and as he set the cup down, he kissed her neck, giving her chills. Kaleigh truly felt like the luckiest woman.

About half an hour later, after finishing her hot chocolate, a text came through on her phone, from Wesley. It had been three weeks since Kaleigh walked into the store and left the note, and now, finally, Wesley was reaching out. She immediately called Jackson over, and together they read: "Hey, Kaleigh, I got your note. I'm sorry it has taken so long to reply. All of this was more than I could handle at first, but I'm doing OK now."

Jackson and Kaleigh looked at each other, and Kaleigh smiled as Jackson put his arms around her. She was happy that her brother had decided to reach out to her. Now all she needed to do was figure out her reply. She didn't want to text right away, so she finished her schoolwork for the night and met Jackson on the couch in front of the fireplace.

The two talked and came up with a reply to Wesley's message.

"I'd love to get together to catch up and see how you are doing. I have missed you." Can you meet sometime this weekend?" Kaleigh sent the message, and now it was time to wait.

It was two days later, while Kaleigh was at school, that Wesley's reply came. "Yeah, we can meet. How about just you and me at Rita's, tonight at six?"

Kaleigh immediately replied, "Yes, I will be there." Then she texted Jackson to tell him she was meeting Wesley alone at the bar.

Jackson called her when he knew school had ended and, after asking about her day, added, "Do you want me to be there tonight?"

"No, Wes requested just me. I can handle it, but I will text you if I need anything." Kaleigh knew Jackson would offer to come, that he would want to be there, but she knew she had to honor Wesley's request. For some reason she felt calm about the meeting. She wasn't sure if it was because of Wesley's kind text messages, or if it was because she knew that deep down her brother was a nice guy. He always had a gentle, funny, sweet way about him, at least he used to, and she was hopeful that someday the two could get back what they had.

The conversation with Jackson continued, "Please call me as soon as you're done. You know I will be worrying about you the whole time." Jackson was always completely honest about his feelings when it came to Kaleigh. And she knew he would be wondering how things were going and worrying about her the entire time. Nothing about his worry was annoying to her at all. In fact, it was his worry, his caring, that gave her comfort.

Kaleigh continued, "I know. Thank you for supporting me. I will be fine, and if I need you, I'll call or text you. I promise. And I'll call as soon as Wes leaves. I love you." Kaleigh truly appreciated her Jackson and always made sure to say "I love you" to him every day, even on the days they didn't see each other.

And with that, Jackson replied, "Love you too," as he hung up the phone.

****

Kaleigh entered the bar first, ordered a drink, and found a quiet high-top table that was off to the side and away from the noise of those at the bar. She made sure to have a view of the front door so that she could wave to Wesley when he came in. He was five minutes late, but Kaleigh was just happy he showed. He waved back, stopped at the bar to grab his drink, and walked over to her.

Kaleigh was sure it was probably too soon for a hug, so she stayed in her seat and simply said, "Hello." Wesley set his beer down on the table and had a seat across from her.

"I've missed you so much, brother."

"Missed you too," Wesley replied in a quiet, maybe a bit hesitant, voice.

The two of them talked about what each had been up to lately, and neither brought up the store or the will at first. Wesley shared how Jackson had told him that the two were together and that he was happy for them. Kaleigh told him how she had noticed the photo of him with a girl on his desk at work. Her brother seemed hesitant to share too much with Kaleigh at first. It was as if he wasn't sure how personal to get with the conversation. He replied with a simple, "Yeah," then stayed quiet, sipping on his beer.

Kaleigh decided to change the subject and told him about their cousin Lola and her baby. She shared the short version of the story, as she wasn't sure how much Wesley wanted to know. He stayed quiet for most of the time as Kaleigh spoke. When she was done, he paused, then said, "I can't remember the last time we saw her, I saw her."

"I think it was probably at Aunt Sara's funeral, a couple years before mom passed." she answered. And, suddenly, with the mention of mom, things became real quiet. Kaleigh let the quiet be for a few moments, then decided to change the subject. "So, how are you?"

Wesley waited, took another sip of his drink, then began, "I'm OK. The store is my whole life, but I hired a girl to manage the registers and cashiers after Dad passed. Her name is Katie. She is really amazing and has taken a lot off of my shoulders. We started dating four months ago. She makes me happy, especially with her sense of humor. I guess I needed some of that in my life," he said as he chuckled.

"That is so great, Wes. I'm so happy for you." Kaleigh was hoping that the happiness she felt for him was coming through in her voice.

Again, there was quiet. A waitress came by and asked if they wanted menus. Wesley quickly said, "No thanks."

Kaleigh wasn't sure why he had said "no" to menus so quickly, but decided to let it go. She was nervous at this moment, about bringing up her involvement in the store, but she needed to know. She had to ask. She was not planning on bringing up the will, but she needed to begin to figure out her place at the store. It had been months since the court date and almost a year since Dad had passed away. The two were now fifty-fifty owners of the store, and she felt like she could not sit on the sidelines anymore.

She began, "So, I've been wanting to ask you, what can I do to help out at the store?" And after this question left her mouth there were crickets. It was as if the entire bar suddenly became quiet.

Wesley didn't say anything. So Kaleigh continued, "I want to help you, Wesley. I mean, I am part owner, I have a history with the store, just like you, and I want to be a part of its future." She worked very hard to speak calmly, making sure that her genuine feelings would shine through. Kaleigh was not frustrated at this moment, but she deeply cared about the store and her brother and wanted this to show in the way she spoke.

Wesley took his hands away from his drink, sat upright, moved closer to the table and to Kaleigh, and said, "You haven't been able to help at the store in forever. It has always been me picking up the pieces, scheduling, ordering, solving problems, and working the fields. You haven't been anywhere to be seen, and now you want to jump in and help? Geez, Kaleigh, I think I'm doing all right on my own." His words were firm, not loud, but firm and clearly upset, and it hurt. It hurt Kaleigh deeply. She fought back a tear at this moment, took a breath and tried to stay calm as she replied:

"Wesley, did you forget that I was taking care of Dad and all of his needs, his issues? Do you realize how much time it took to care for him at the house when his memory began to fade, then move him to Havenwood, and sell the house? Have you thought of that? All of that took up my extra time for months and months before Dad died. That is what I was doing. I'm sorry I didn't have anything else to give to the store, but now I can." Kaleigh tried very hard to keep calm and state the facts in a nice way, avoiding defensiveness. "I know that you had as much work to do as I did, and I realize that you may not have realized all I did to keep dad going, to make sure he had what he needed, that he was in the safest place. And I probably don't fully understand everything you had to do to keep the store going and thriving. But I want to work to understand so that we can get back the relationship we had," and she paused just a moment before adding, "before mom died."

At that moment, Wesley got up, took some cash out of his wallet and threw it on the table.

"So that's it? That's how you want to leave things between us?" Kaleigh was disappointed that her brother had given up on the conversation.

"Yeah, I'm doing just fine. I gotta go," he said, pushing in his chair before walking away.

"Ugh," Kaleigh said as she slumped back in her chair. "And to think that our conversation was going so well," she said to herself as she took another sip of her drink. Then she called Jackson. "I'll meet you at your place," he replied when she told him that Wesley had walked out on her.

When Kaleigh walked in the door, she decided to take a quick shower and change into more comfortable clothes. Jackson had a key so he could let himself in. He started by turning on her fireplace, finding plates, and putting the pizza he had picked up on the coffee table. When he saw Kaleigh walk from her closet back into her bathroom, he walked over and stood in the doorway. As she hung up her towel, her eye caught Jackson in the mirror. She turned around, and before she knew it, she was inside Jackson's arms, bawling.

Jackson knew she needed time and space and that she would share the story of tonight when she was ready. Kaleigh gently took his hand and pulled him into the bathroom so she could reach her hairbrush, then she led him to the couch. Without a word, he took the hairbrush from her hand and slowly brushed her hair. He had never done that before, but it felt so good. Kaleigh closed her eyes and just relaxed. When he was done, she turned toward him, slowly moved closer, and they kissed. One kiss from Jackson always seemed to be able to calm her nerves and make her heart race all at the same time. It was magic.

It wasn't until after Kaleigh had a few bites of pizza that she had the energy to tell the story. She told Jackson of the entire conversation—from the updates on their personal lives, which went well, and then how everything changed the minute she wanted to talk about the store.

"I had to bring up the store, Jackson. It's my legacy, too," Kaleigh said as she leaned against him on the couch.

"I know. Hopefully, he will come around. I know it doesn't feel like it, but I think this was the beginning of the conversation that needed to happen. I feel like it is progress. He just needs more time, I guess. I know it is hard, but if you can let go of the hurt for a while and focus on your life, maybe this one conversation won't have to ruin these next few weeks." Jackson always had clarity and patience, which is one of the reasons she loved him.

"I guess I just don't understand. I explained how much I had to do for dad and I told him that I probably didn't understand how much he had to do at the store. But I told him I wanted to help now, that I wanted to understand what he has been through. And it's true, I do want to understand. He just didn't want to hear any more. It's as if his mind was closed to the idea." Kaleigh's voice was soft and quiet. She sat there quietly for a moment with her eyes closed, then realized the knot in her stomach. She needed something fizzy for her stomach and walked over to the kitchen. Upon taking a clear soda out of the fridge, she looked at Jackson and said, "What are you drinking?"

"I'll have what you're having," he replied, making her smile.

The two finished their dinner and decided there wasn't anything left to do now but to wait and to give Wesley more time. Kaleigh realized that Jackson was probably right. There was no use letting the anger and the frustration ruin the next weeks or months to come. Taking a deep breath, moving on with her life, and giving Wesley his space was the best thing to do.

CHAPTER 25

It was a busy December. The eighth graders who would soon be leaving their school had concerts that they always wanted Kaleigh and Danielle to attend. The two were very high on the list of favorite teachers at their school. They always enjoyed seeing the hard work of their students outside of their classrooms and were very proud of their accomplishments. After the concerts, both teachers seemed to be celebrities as many students found them after the show. No autographs were exchanged, but there were plenty of hugs and photos. These concerts definitely made for some fun nights this time of year.

There was also a Christmas party for the staff at Lola's daycare center. It was on a Friday evening and Kaleigh had offered to watch Hannah so that Lola could attend the fun event. Jackson had come too and they brought Hannah her Christmas presents, as they would be on their trip to Texas when the holidays came.

Lola didn't stay very late at the party. She was happy to attend the event but wanted to spend a little time with Jackson and Kaleigh before they had to drive home. She loved any chance to spend with her new family and enjoyed getting to know Jackson better. Lola wanted to have some time to talk to them for a bit when Hannah was asleep.

In their conversation Lola shared that she had sent one more note to Ryan's parents more than a month ago, but that she wasn't holding her breath that things would change. Lola mentioned that this last letter was more for her than them, as she needed to move on from the sadness, to move past the worry that she had not done enough, tried hard enough. She wanted to get the last of her thoughts off of her chest so that she could truly move on with her new life. Lola said that the day she mailed the letter she did feel as if some weight had been lifted off her shoulders. "The ball is in their court, it is their decision now, to be or to not be a part of their grand-daughter's life. I have done everything, said everything that I could. Now I can let go and just let things happen as they are supposed to."

"I am proud of you, putting your heart out there one more time. I don't know of many people who would go to the trouble of reaching out again, asking one more time for someone to care, who hasn't shown a breath of that the entire time." Lola appreciated her cousin's words and she felt good. She felt like her path had led her to this place, this perfect fresh start. Her job was a perfect fit for her, and the center was perfect for Hannah. The precious girl was growing at a good pace, meeting all of her milestones and had no sign of any breathing problems, which was a great relief to Lola.

Kaleigh was so happy for her cousin, that her life path had turned toward the positive and that everything was going so well. Both cousins were happy for each other and shared many hugs before the night was over. Before Kaleigh said goodbye she gave Lola her Christmas gift but told her she should wait to open it, giving her something special to open on the holiday. Inside the gold-wrapped box was a gift card to the local grocery store, a kit to make Hannah's handprint, and a locket for Lola, with a photo of Ryan and Hannah inside. Kaleigh felt like these gifts would help make this Christmas a special one for her cousins, even though Jackson and Kaleigh couldn't be there to celebrate with them.

****

It was one week before Christmas when Danielle texted Kaleigh, saying they were headed to the hospital with the baby on the way! Kaleigh was so excited for her best friend and asked Chris to keep her posted on the progress. The next day Kaleigh found herself on her way to the hospital to meet little Cara Eleanor. She was so tiny, so soft, and so beautiful. Chris took a picture of Kaleigh holding little Cara, which was sent to Jackson an hour later. Upon seeing the photo on his phone, Jackson found his heart warming as he pictured Kaleigh someday holding their child. She would make such an amazing mother, he thought. And Kaleigh knew that someday Jackson would make an amazing father too. As for now, she was over the moon with happiness for her best friend and her new baby girl!

Soon after came the trip to Texas for Jeremy's wedding. Jackson spent more time packing for the trip than he usually did, as the plan was to drive there in his truck and he wanted to be prepared for anything. He packed a cooler with drinks, a bag with extra jackets, rain gear, blankets, and the normal emergency gear in case the battery or tires needed attention. He also had to decide what to wear for the various events leading up to the wedding, so he packed his suitcase accordingly. And most importantly, there was the small box from the jewelry store.

That day on the beach, when Jackson had slipped away for a few minutes, he had found the perfect ring for Kaleigh. Ever since the day Kaleigh had come to him, he had pictured himself getting down on one knee, asking her to marry him. However, in all his dreams he could never picture the setting, the where or the when, in his mind. He was sure about one thing, that he wanted to ask her to marry him, and soon. It's not that he was impatient, but that he felt they had wasted so much time in all those years they weren't together. Jackson didn't want to waste any more time before making things official. His goal on this trip to Texas was to find the perfect time and place to ask her. Jackson was hopeful that he would just know when the time was right. He didn't want the added pressure of trying to plan the perfect moment, when an unplanned, organic, beautiful moment would be more special. This mindset helped him stay relaxed, though he couldn't help but feel a slight bit of nervousness, as he imagined everyone felt in this huge life moment. The one thing he did do, was to make sure that the jackets, the flannels, and the suit coats he chose had a good pocket for the jewelry box. That, he felt, was the key to his spontaneity.

On the way to the wedding, they spent one very long day driving so that the second day they would have time to relax at the hotel before the rehearsal dinner. The hotel they stayed at on the first night was a simple one and did not have a restaurant. They asked the clerk for his recommendation, and he told them of a great Mexican place just down the street. Jackson and Kaleigh looked at each other and smiled, each knowing that would be the perfect choice. The front of the restaurant looked plain, but the interior gave the impression of walking the streets of Mexico.

After following the hostess through a narrow archway, they followed a long winding pathway, complete with twinkling lights and small, intimate tables. The lights reminded both of the street fair back home, and the table they were given was around the corner, near a fountain, in a slightly secluded area. It was perfect. Kaleigh had freshened up at the hotel and was wearing a flowy dress and lavender sweater, while Jackson wore a new pair of jeans, a nice button-down shirt and a jacket. The dinner was wonderful, the company and conversation amazing as always, and Jackson decided this was the moment.

When the waitress cleared their plates, before their churros arrived at the table, he stood up and held out his hand. He pulled her gently up from her seat and brought her a few steps closer to the fountain. The twinkling lights were above them, and a soft breeze from a fan moved her hair as he touched her face. It made for the most lovely, private, beautiful moment.

Jackson began, "Leigh, I have waited so long for you that every day I wake up, I have to pinch myself. Did my dream really come true? Is she really mine? Kaleigh, you make my heart so happy, and I am so grateful for you every day." Kaleigh was beginning to tremble, not in fear but in excitement, in happiness. Was this really what she thought it was? Was this really happening?

Then Jackson continued, "I am so in love with you, and I picture our life together. I want to spend the rest of my life with you, through the happy times and the sad ones. I want to be with you through it all. Kaleigh… will you do me the honor of becoming my wife?"

There it was. And at that moment, a tear came to Kaleigh's cheek.

"Will you marry me?" And as Jackson said these words, he wiped her tear away from her cheek, slowly reached into his pocket, got down on one knee, and opened the box. Kaleigh didn't care what the ring looked like. She knew what her answer was, but she couldn't help but look at the small, shiny, perfect diamond in a silver setting. The tears continued to flow faster down her cheeks now, and she trembled, smiled, and said, "Yes, yes, I'll marry you!" And she bent down to give him a kiss. The two stood up and embraced before Jackson had a moment to put the ring on her finger. Then he wiped the tears from her eyes and gave her a long, soft kiss. The moment was better than Jackson could have imagined, could have planned. It was amazing!

The two took a few more minutes by the fountain, Kaleigh inside of Jackson's arms, both swaying to the beat of the quiet music playing. Neither one wanted the moment to end, each taking a mental picture of their surroundings and each other, not wanting to ever forget this night. When the waitress came back with their desserts, she offered to take their picture and Kaleigh knew that this photo would join the other special moments of her life on her bookshelf.

Later that night, Kaleigh sent a picture of the ring to Danielle, who let out a scream of excitement that startled Chris at first. Danielle was incredibly thrilled for her friend. The return text made Kaleigh laugh as it was a picture of baby Cara, seeming to be holding a paper that said, "Congratulations K + J." She had wished for this moment for her best friend for so long, and now, it had finally happened.

Jeremy and Jenny's rehearsal dinner was at a beautiful farm, on a deck overlooking farmland, with a DJ and such great company. Kaleigh remembered Jeremy's parents from her college days, and they had some great conversations in between dancing and enjoying delicious food.

The wedding took place in a quaint white church. It was the kind you see in movies—small but beautiful. Jenny, the bride, was stunning in a simple white dress, and when Jeremy said, "I do," Jackson squeezed Kaleigh's hand, then leaned over and kissed her on the cheek, imagining the moment he would get to say that to her. Kaleigh's heart fluttered at that moment as she turned to look at Jackson and then back at the bride and groom. Upon leaving the church, the guests blew bubbles and waved sparklers as everyone cheered the new couple. Kaleigh was so happy that she didn't miss this special occasion. She was even more happy that Jackson was able to share this memory with her.

There was an hour in between the ceremony and the reception and Jackson and Kaleigh found a river with a pathway to walk along. It was a beautiful day to be walking with your soul mate, your true love. The two spoke about what they hoped their wedding day would be like and agreed the simpler, the smaller, the better. Neither one had a date in mind, that would come in time, but were so in love and felt lucky to have found each other.

Jenny was amazing and perfect for Jeremy. The two had such chemistry and would often finish each other's sentences. When there was a problem with the flowers at the reception, she was so cool and graceful as she solved it. Jeremy held her hand most of the night, and each time they made each other laugh, it warmed Kaleigh's heart. She was so truly happy for her friend. The small size of the wedding was perfect, giving the four of them time to sit and talk after dinner was finished. This was what Kaleigh envisioned for their special day, a very small guest list with time to sit and talk to friends and family. The simplicity of the day allowed for such a relaxing atmosphere and was just amazing. It allowed the two to get know Jenny more, and as they sat and talked together, Kaleigh became more convinced that she and Jeremy were meant to be.

It took Jeremy only about five minutes to notice the ring on Kaleigh's finger. He stopped in mid-sentence, put his hand near Kaleigh's, which was resting on the table, looked up at her and Jackson and said, "Is this what I think it is?" His voice was in complete excitement and Kaleigh smiled, "Yes, it is!" And at that moment Jeremy and Kaleigh stood up and embraced each other. Jeremy then shook Jackson's hand and pulled him in for a hug. Then the two shared the story of the romantic night at the Mexican Restaurant. Jenny went to get four glasses of champagne, and they made a toast to the finding of true love and to their futures. Kaleigh realized again how lucky she was and how truly perfect this entire trip had been.

It was when the reception was winding down when Kaleigh's phone rang. It was a number she didn't recognize, so she let it go to voicemail. Jackson took Kaleigh to the dance floor for one more slow dance. The tenderness with which Jackson held her as they rocked from side to side reminded both of them of the first night away at the beach hotel. The first night they shared everything with each other. The night Kaleigh had walked toward him in her nightgown, and he had taken her in his arms, slow dancing with her as if there was music. Kaleigh also remembered that night as they danced, putting her head on his shoulder, realizing that, just a few months ago, this moment was extremely difficult for her to picture. Moving from those broken feelings to now this was a miracle, and Kaleigh was extremely grateful.

After the song ended, the two said goodbye to Jeremy and Jenny, thanking them for such a wonderful evening. They had enjoyed their time in Texas, and both thanked Jeremy for being such a wonderful friend. The four decided that they should meet somewhere in the summertime and spend some more time together. Even Jackson liked that idea. He appreciated Jeremy so much and enjoyed his company. Any feelings of jealousy had melted away and he loved going on vacation with Kaleigh. Jenny volunteered to do the research and send options of get-away spots.

As the girls walked ahead, Jackson stayed back a moment to talk to Jeremy in private. "Hey, thanks again for helping Leigh through that difficult time when I wasn't around. I really messed up."

"Not a problem at all. You know love makes us crazy." Jeremy smiled as he shook Jackson's hand once more, then continued. "She is an amazing friend and I enjoy our conversations. That week of the funeral . . . I'm sorry if I gave you the wrong idea about us."

Jackson continued, "Yeah, Kaleigh told me that you were just friends, but my heart was a mess that week. I was a jerk for leaving her alone so long. You were there for her and helped give her the courage to come find me. I can't thank you enough for that." Jackson was glad he had a moment to share that with him, and the two men shook hands again and then pulled in for a hug.

"I'm so glad that it worked out," Jeremy replied. "I knew there was something more, something special between you. I'm so happy for you both."

"Thank you. Congratulations again," Jackson replied as the two walked toward the door.

"Congratulations to you too!" Jeremy added before catching up to Kaleigh and giving her one last hug to say goodbye. They took one more selfie of the four of them before Jackson took Kaleigh's hand and walked her to the truck.

The minute Jackson opened the door of the truck for Kaleigh, her phone rang again. Looking at the list of missed calls, she realized that this number had called her three times in the past thirty minutes. She gave a worried look to Jackson, then decided to answer the call.

For some reason as her hand touched the screen, she felt a lump in her chest. She would one day realize that this call would change their lives forever.

CHAPTER 26

On the other end of the line was a woman's voice. "Hi, I'm looking for a family member of Lola Sullivan."

Kaleigh's heart sank in this moment, so low it felt like it was in her stomach. There was no way this could be good.

After a moment she got herself together and replied: "Umm, yes, I am her cousin, Kaleigh Evans."

"There has been a horrible accident, and we need you to come to Hanover General Hospital right away." Kaleigh was right to feel her heart sinking, her mind racing as to what could have happened. She rubber her head over her left eye then spoke.

"Oh, no, I mean, I'm out of town. I'm in Texas." Kaleigh's mind was moving a mile a minute. What could have happened? How can I get home quickly? What am I supposed to do? Jackson had gotten in the driver's seat by this point but had not turned on the truck. He turned to face Kaleigh and mouthed the words, "What's wrong?"

Kaleigh whispered back, "There's been some kind of accident . . . with Lola."

The woman on the other end of the line continued, "Do you know if she has anyone else in the area, any other family?"

"No, she has no other family." Kaleigh began, her mind continuing to race, then it came to her, "I can send two friends in my place until I can get there, well three actually." Her mind went to Danielle, Chris, and then to Sandra. I can be there the day after tomorrow. We have to drive from Texas." And then, even though she was scared to ask, she continued, "Can I ask what happened?"

"She was in a car accident and is in critical condition. They are preparing her for surgery, but things aren't looking good." The nurse spoke with a gentle tone, knowing that this would be difficult to hear.

As if a light switch went on in her brain, Kaleigh rushed the words, "What about the baby, Hannah? Was she in the car?" Kaleigh's heart was racing even more now at the thought of the baby being hurt.

"Yes, she was in the car. She is here too and looks to have a broken arm but is doing well. They continue to monitor her closely, but she is stable and awake." And as these words came to Kaleigh, tears began to fall.

She took a moment to catch her breath and said, "Can I send our friend, Danielle Miller, to be with Hannah? She knows the baby very well. I don't want Hannah to be alone. Can she have an adult with her?" She couldn't imagine being so little and being alone in a strange place. It was hard enough when this happened as an adult.

"Absolutely! Let me put her name in the system so the staff knows," the woman continued in her caring voice.

"And Chris Miller and Sandra Lann, can they be on the list for Hannah until I can get there? Sandra is the director of her daycare center and knows her well."

"Sure," she replied and took a moment to get the correct spellings and information. The tears continued to fall for Kaleigh. There was nothing she could do at this moment to stop them. "Who will call me with an update on Lola, or is there a number I can call?" Even in this emotional state, she thought to ask these important questions. "And how did you find me?"

The woman on the other line gave Kaleigh the best phone number to call, and Jackson had thought to open his phone at this moment so he could text the number to Kaleigh. Kaleigh switched the phone to speaker so he could hear. She also said that when Lola came out of surgery, one of the nurses would call her with an update. As for the last question, she replied, "The police on the scene recovered her cell phone and gave it to me to try and find someone who was related to her. Your phone number was at the top of the list, so you're the first one I called."

"Thank you. And please tell Hannah that 'Lai-Lai' is coming."

"I will. Drive safely, and we will talk soon," the nurse said before hanging up the phone.

And before Kaleigh knew it, she had jumped over into Jackson's arms once again. She was quiet for a minute, just enjoying the warmth of his arms as all of this had given her the chills. Then she went over everything the nurse had told her. Kaleigh was still crying and didn't think she could handle explaining things again. So they came up with a plan: Kaleigh would text the story to Sandra while Jackson would call Danielle. He would ask if she and Chris could take turns at the hospital with Sandra until they could get there.

Once they took care of contacting the support system, the two decided they would pack up their things at the hotel and begin driving tonight. If they took turns driving and sleeping, maybe they could drive straight through. Danielle and Chris absolutely were on board with the plan and would take turns being home with their newborn and at the hospital with Hannah. They were as shocked as Kaleigh and Jackson were with the tragic event that had taken place and wanted to do anything they could to help Hannah.

****

Exhaustion had set in about twelve hours into the trip home, so the two pulled over at a rest stop, and both slept. When they awoke, they kissed for a moment, then went inside to freshen up, grab breakfast and some fresh coffee. This break in the trip gave them the much-needed energy to keep going. The combination of lack of sleep, crazy emotions, and unanswered questions depleted Kaleigh's energy faster than ever.

She had received one phone call from a different nurse once Lola's surgery was over. The nurse explained that they still had Lola listed in critical condition, and they were having trouble stabilizing her vitals. She had a nurse in her room the entire time, and they had her on oxygen. She were in the process of putting Lola in a medically induced coma to try to alleviate any more swelling. The car that hit her had crashed into the driver's side in a T-bone crash. Fortunately, Hannah was in the backseat on the opposite side and only suffered a broken arm. Despite this, the nurse reported that Hannah was in good spirits.

In the last few hours Danielle had given Kaleigh an update and sent her some photos of Hannah. In one photo, Hannah was squeezing a teddy bear that Danielle had brought her, while in another, Chris and Hannah were seen eating ice cream and smiling together. Hannah's smile made her happy for a moment in the sea of sadness that was raging inside of her. Kaleigh wanted to be there with Hannah at this moment, but they still had a long way to drive. The feeling of helplessness continued, though having Danielle and Chris with Hannah eased the helpless feelings a little. Sandra had also come to the hospital and took the overnight shift so that the new parents could be home and get some sleep.

When Jackson and Kaleigh were three hours away, Sandra called to give an update on Lola. "It isn't looking good," she began when Kaleigh asked how she was. "She has a lot of internal bleeding, and her brain is swollen from the trauma. They want to take her out of the coma in a couple of days to see how and if her body will begin the healing process on its own. Lola also has two arm fractures and a leg fracture. Those are cast already, and she is badly bruised. They are really worried about her brain now. It's just so heartbreaking. They said it was a drunk driver that hit her."

Kaleigh had the phone on speaker, so Jackson could hear everything that was said. Tears came to her eyes yet again, and Jackson reached over to squeeze her hand. It seemed like Jackson had been doing that a lot lately. He was her rock, and she could not imagine going through this without him. They both thanked Sandra for all her help through this. She told them, "I wouldn't want to be anywhere else right now. And Hannah, she is all smiles with her visitors. The nurses chipped in to buy her a new blanket and a couple of toys to keep her occupied. She can go home soon. I think they are waiting for you to get here, and then they will discharge her."

"Yes, I will take care of her, definitely. Can you tell the nurses that we should be there in about three hours? And will you be able to let me into Lola's house so I can pick up some things?" For the first time in this long journey, Kaleigh found herself able to think somewhat clearly.

"Absolutely," Sandra replied before hanging up the phone. Kaleigh was lucky to have this support system when she was so far away from home.

When Kaleigh hung up the phone, Jackson said, "I am here for you, Kaleigh. I will help with Hannah as much as I can."

"Thank you, Jackson. I don't know what I would do without you. I guess we will have to figure out our new normal once again."

"You could move in with me. I mean, I don't want to rush things if you're not ready, but whenever you are I want to be. You and Hannah could stay with me, even if I have to rearrange the whole house, I wouldn't mind at all." Jackson truly meant it, and Kaleigh knew that he did. Jackson would never say anything that he didn't truly mean. "Or, if it is easier for the two of you to be at your place, I can come stay the night more, to help. Whatever you need, Leigh." Jackson really meant what he said, that he would be there for her through anything and would never leave her, and in this moment, Kaleigh felt it.

"Gosh, yes, that might make things easier, but I need to see how everything will play out. I need to talk to Danielle and see if she can help with childcare. You and I still need to work. Between the three of us, maybe we can make a decent plan. I am not sure where the best place will be, but let's figure this out together. I appreciate you so much, Jackson!"

****

The hospital gave temporary custody of Hannah to Kaleigh. Before picking the little girl up from the hospital, they met Sandra at Lola's house and picked up food, toys, clothes, and the travel crib. They also stopped at the discount store to pick up two car seats, one for Kaleigh's car and one for Jackson's. He insisted on having one so that he could drive her around and be more of a help. They chose some food items that would be helpful and could be kept in the car for a while. Jackson planned to get milk and eggs later, after they got home.

Kaleigh brought the nurses who cared for Lola and Hannah flowers. She was incredible grateful for all they had done while she was so far away. After picking up Hannah from the hospital, the two drove to Danielle's house. They decided that was the most important place to be, with friends, and Chris went out to get dinner as the three of them talked. This news, these developments in the game of life, had taken them all by surprise. No one could have imagined the story as it was playing out. Jackson and Kaleigh shared their deep appreciation for Chris and Danielle for all they did these past few days to help Hannah feel safe and happy. The friends shared that they would not have wanted to be anywhere else.

It wasn't until Kaleigh reached for her second piece of pizza that Danielle reached for Kaleigh's ringed hand. "With all of the worry about Lola and Hannah, I almost forgot you got engaged!"

Kaleigh smiled and said, "Yes!" The two held each other in a deep embrace, with laughter at first, then tears. The tears were partially happy and partially sad. Kaleigh had tried to keep herself together since they drove into town, her eyes puffy with all the crying she had done on the trip back. But here, in her friend's arms, the tears came again.

"Why are you crying?" Danielle said as she wiped a tear from Kaleigh's cheek.

"I am so happy for my life ahead with the best man I have ever known, but I just can't hold the emotions in for our Hannah and Lola. I still can't believe what has happened, and I am worried about how we will juggle everything. I have to go back to work next week, and poor Hannah, has already lost her father, and now . . ."

Danielle interrupted her, "Hold on, let's just take one day at a time and pray that Lola will come out of this. We can all pitch in, we can all help Hannah in the meantime. I am home with the baby anyway, so you can drop Hannah off here as much as you need to." Danielle was so calm through all of this and her words helped settle Kaleigh's nerves a bit.

"We are all a team and will all help with Hannah. It doesn't have to be all on your shoulders. That's why I bought the extra car seat. I am hear for you Leigh, we are hear for you." Jackson and Danielle's words warmed her heart and calmed her down a bit.

Danielle brushed Kaleigh's hair away from her face as Kaleigh began, "I can't ask you to . . ."

Danielle interrupted her. "We won't take no for an answer. It is no trouble at all." And just like that, childcare was taken care of. The friends ate dinner and talked for another hour, then decided it was time to get Hannah home. Chris and Danielle had a new appreciation for Jackson, seeing him in action, helping Hannah and Kaleigh with whatever they needed. And the four decided that once a week throughout this ordeal, they would have dinner around the kitchen island together. Kaleigh appreciated her best friend immensely and they were beginning to feel like her very own extended family.

****

The next day Jackson took care of Hannah for a few hours as Kaleigh was given permission to sit with Lola in her hospital bed. They were going to lift her from her coma and Kaleigh wanted to be there to hold her hand. She was still listed in critical condition. As she sat there, quietly at first, she thought of the memories she had with her cousin and how much she appreciated Lola coming back into her life just when she needed someone to lean on. After reminiscing about the past few months in her mind, she finally began to speak. Kaleigh updated Lola on Hannah's condition, saying that although she had a broken arm, she was always in good spirits, being spoiled by the nurses and their friends. She told her how her daughter had enjoyed ice cream treats every day and was given new toys to play with. Kaleigh reassured her that she would take care of Hannah until she got back on her feet, telling her not to worry. Then she found herself confiding in Lola how much she truly appreciated her knocking on her door all those months ago. She told her how low she felt in her life at that moment, how alone she was, and that she could not thank her enough for bringing a bright spot to her life when she and Hannah moved in for a while. She let Lola know that she would always be grateful for that as she squeezed her hand and wiped a tear from her eye.

An hour later, with tears still streaming down her face, she kissed Lola's hand, told her to stay strong and keep fighting. Kaleigh hoped that her words would give Lola the confidence that she could conquer this trauma and share how much she loved her.

Kaleigh had stayed for over two hours with Lola, not leaving out her happy news of her engagement to Jackson. She had heard that even people in comas can hear what people were saying. Kaleigh hoped that Lola could hear her voice and everything that was said.

Upon walking out of the hospital room, she decided to stop at the coffee shop to grab a cup of warm coffee. While waiting at the counter for her coffee to be made, she noticed Wesley. At first Kaleigh thought she was seeing things, but looking again she realized it was in fact her brother. He was sitting in the large waiting area next to the coffee shop, running his hand through his hair, like he did when he was nervous. Shocked to see her brother here, she missed the barista calling her name the first time. As they called her name again, she snapped out of her fog, took her cup of coffee, and walked over to Wesley.

He was sitting upright, but slouched a little, his elbows resting on his legs, his eyes looking down at the ground. There was a seat to the side of him open, and without saying a word, she sat down and put her hand on her brother's shoulder. At that moment, Wesley looked up, surprised to see his sister there. Kaleigh reached over and gave his hand a light squeeze. She immediately noticed his face, sad and showing lack of sleep. He noticed her face, sad and puffy as it she had been crying for an hour.

After a slight pause, at the same time they asked each other, "What's wrong?"

Wesley's voice was more gentle and caring than she had heard it in a long time. He seemed to truly care about why Kaleigh was here and what was causing her such sadness. Kaleigh told him the story of Lola and Hannah and how worried and nervous she was about Lola's condition. The selfishness had melted away and Wesley truly cared about what his sister was going through at this moment.

"Wow, I'm so sorry, Kaleigh. I hope she is going to be OK."

"Me too," Kaleigh replied, taking her napkin and wiping another tear from her cheek. Then she turned her attention to him, "What about you? What are you doing here?"

Wesley went on to talk about his girlfriend, Katie, who had taken a bad fall and broken her leg in two places. They were also monitoring her for a concussion. She had not fallen at work but at her dad's house while she was trying to help him with a project. Wesley regretted not going with her to help them as she had originally asked him to do. He did not share this fact with Kaleigh, but instead continued, "I should've been there," he said. "I've been so focused on me, on my list of things to do, on my emotions, that I haven't been open to see what anyone else needs, what anyone else is feeling." He paused, noticing that Kaleigh's hand was still on top of his. "She has been in surgery for so long that I had to get out of that tiny waiting room, and I have just been replaying the past couple of years in my head, over and over. It's like this event, this accident is like a wake-up call, Katie's fall." He paused as he ran his fingers through his hair again. "She is so great, and I have started to take time to relax with her, you know, take some time away from the store. I know I need a break, a life outside the store, it's just hard."

After a few moments he added, "I should've been there. I could have . . ." and at this moment Kaleigh interrupted. "Wesley, don't. Don't put this on yourself. I did that with Dad for a while, remember? I was kicking myself for not cancelling my observation and going to be with Dad. It is no use. We can't prevent everything. What is meant to happen, will find a way anyway. You can't beat yourself up over this."

Kaleigh wasn't sure if she had said too much. She decided to stay quiet, to not say anything, to just let him speak. "I don't know what she sees in me. I know I have been so stuck lately. She is such a great girl and she is a huge help at the store." He paused for another moment. "She asked me to come to her dad's and I let her down."

Carefully, Kaleigh replied, "I'm sure that she understood that you couldn't come to help her. She knows the store keeps you so busy." Then she got quiet again.

"If I would have been there for her, this wouldn't have happened." Wesley added.

"I know it seems like that now, but you never know how the events would have unfolded. Maybe it would have been you that took a bad fall. You have to forgive yourself Wesley. I know it will take time, but you have to. It took me a while to forgive myself for not being there for Dad that day. I just kept thinking, if I would have changed my observation, if I would have taken a half day, then maybe I would have been there, kept him from taking a nap after lunch, that, maybe we wouldn't have lost him that day. But, then he may have passed away during his nap a day or two later. I couldn't be with him all day every day. Wesley, you can't beat yourself up for this. You can't change what has happened. And blaming yourself won't change anything." After these words, Kaleigh got quiet again.

They each sat quietly for almost five minutes, just sipping on their coffees and thinking. Kaleigh had taken her hand away from

Wesley's but didn't feel that it was time for her to leave yet. She felt from Wesley's body language that he was glad she was there. Then the words came. The words Kaleigh had been hoping would be said for some time now.

"I'm sorry." Wesley spoke in a quiet, but meaningful tone.

Kaleigh, in this moment did not know what to say. She had hoped to hear the words from her brother someday but never rehearsed what she would say. All she could do was look in his eyes, a tear coming to her cheek and suddenly she found herself embracing her brother. She could feel him bring his arms around her like he hadn't done in years. Kaleigh, only being able to muster a whisper voice replied, "I'm sorry too," as they continued to hug for a minute more.

A few minutes later Kaleigh talked Wesley into letting her buy him a fresh cup of coffee and taking a walk. They decided that starting a once-a-week family dinner would be a good place to begin rebuilding their relationship. Wesley apologized at least twice during their walk for being such a jerk, and Kaleigh told him how much she appreciated being able to talk to her brother again. "You have always been such a big part of my life Wes, that when you aren't in my life it really feels as if there is a hole. I know I must sound weird."

"No," Wesley replied, "Not at all."

They agreed that they would talk soon and that Sunday nights seemed like a good night for family dinners. Wesley said that he wanted to try closing at four on Sundays to give himself and the employees more family time at the end of the week.

Kaleigh decided not to bring up anything more about the Garden Center, that all of that would come in time. Wesley wasn't sure what Katie's recovery would be like but he shared with Kaleigh that he wanted to be there for her through it all. It seemed to her that, with this accident, his eyes had opened up to see what was truly important to him, and how his vision was clouded for such a long time as he only thought about himself. No one wants these bad accidents to happen, but maybe these events happened to push people in a direction that they are supposed to go. Maybe everything truly did happen for a reason. Not that Kaleigh wished anything bad on anyone, but Katie's fall had been the event that brought her brother back.

"Will you text me updates on Katie? I would like to know how she is doing." Kaleigh asked.

"Yes of course, if you will let me know about Lola?" Wesley's voice was just as caring as she remembered it from what seemed like so long ago.

It was then that Wesley realized that he should get back to the small waiting room. Kaleigh walked him to the entrance of the room and the brother and sister embraced like they had not done in forever, and it felt so nice. "I'm sorry I was such a jerk," he added one more time, then squeezed her hand as Kaleigh replied, "I love you brother," as he turned and walked away.

Kaleigh sat back down in the large waiting room, taking another sip of her coffee, in complete disbelief at what had just happened. What were the odds that she and Wesley would be in the hospital, visiting loved ones at the same time, and that they would begin to heal their relationship on this day, in this place, under these circumstances? The overlapping events that had brought the two together on this day were almost unimaginable. But, their paths had crossed and Wesley was beginning to change, for the better. This proved to Kaleigh that blessings can come out of tragedy. Before Kaleigh stood up to leave, she found herself praying. She prayed for healing for Lola and Katie, and healing for Wesley and for the brother-sister relationship they once had. Kaleigh hadn't been a big prayer person throughout the years. Her parents had not been those kind of people, but as these events unfolded in Kaleigh's life, she was beginning to think that there was a higher power, bringing things together, helping what was meant to be.

Fifteen minutes later, Kaleigh was back in her car, driving to Jackson to tell him the unbelievable news, that she had run into Wesley at the hospital that they had begun their road to healing. Jackson was so very happy for his girl, and had been hoping for a long time that she could have her brother back. Kaleigh deserved that, so much.

****

The news that Kaleigh would get three days later was the worst she could even imagine. The crash had caused Lola such bad brain damage that, even if the rest of her body healed, it would give her absolutely no quality of life, no ability to do anything for herself. Once it was proved that Lola had no other family to contact, to speak for her, it was left to Kaleigh and the doctors to make the decision, the horrible decision, to let her go. And within hours, Lola was gone.

Kaleigh found herself sitting on a bench in the courtyard of the hospital, tears falling like a river after a rain, with her thoughts, her emotions, going directly to Hannah. She would grow up now without a father and without a mother. This was the saddest story for a little girl—orphaned before the age of two. Kaleigh had cried so much in the past week that she thought there wouldn't be any tears left, but without fail, they came.

Jackson was amazing through it all. He quickly became the best dad he could be to Hannah, and she had already melted his heart. She was beginning to talk, and Jackson loved teaching her about all the animals on his farm. They had such an adorable bond.

Kaleigh loved sharing books with Hannah, and the two would go to the library once a week to choose an entire bag of new books to explore at home. They also had playdough and coloring time at the kitchen island as Kaleigh cooked in the kitchen.

The three of them frequented the coffee shop and the local children's museum, finding yet again a new normal for this new family that had been created. A month after Lola had passed, Jackson asked Kaleigh if he could adopt Hannah along with her, together. Kaleigh didn't know why but at first she was taken by surprise. It wasn't as if the conversation between them at this moment was even remotely about Hannah. They were sitting on his porch, while Hannah was taking a nap, talking about the farm. Then, all of a sudden, out of left field he asked, "When you adopt Hannah, can we do it together? I would like to be her dad, and continue raising her with you . . . What do you think?" Kaleigh paused for a moment and could feel a smile come to her face. She jumped into his arms, filled with such happiness that Jackson wanted to be a part of Hannah's life forever and replied with an excited, "Yes!"

A few weeks later, it was official that Jackson Sanders and Kaleigh Evans were now the proud parents of Hannah. The two would always celebrate with Hannah her "Adoption Day," just as they would celebrate Lola's parents, once a year, on the anniversary of when Lola knocked on Kaleigh's door. On that day each year, Jackson, Hannah and Kaleigh would plant flowers next to a plaque that Kaleigh had made, commemorating the love that Ryan and Lola had for Hannah. As for the locket that Kaleigh made for Lola, that was put away in a safe place, and Kaleigh planned on giving it to Hannah on her thirteenth birthday. Kaleigh wanted Hannah to feel like she and Jackson were her mom and dad, but made sure that Hannah would never forget who her birth parents were.

A few months later, on a warm summer day, Kaleigh and Jackson had their small wedding with Hannah and Cara as the flower girls, Wesley as the best man, and Danielle as the maid of honor. The ceremony happened in the gazebo, the same one where Kaleigh had turned down Jackson all those years ago. Kaleigh was determined to have that be a happy place for the two and Jackson loved the idea. The reception was on the same property, under a tent, and was simple, yet magical. Everything was perfect, except for Lola not being there. Kaleigh knew that Lola was there in spirit, as was her Mom and Dad. She knew that they would be so proud of the life, the family she had made.

Katie was there, growing closer to Wesley every day, and was the photographer for the evening. Katie, who had begun to come to Sunday dinners and was an amazing compliment to Wesley, had started to become part of the family. She was recovering nicely from the accident and was such a caring, positive person. It was her that helped Wesley find his softer side and overcome all of the sadness that had brought him down these past few years, and Kaleigh was grateful for that.

Instead of the father-daughter dance, it was the brother-sister dance, and Kaleigh was so happy in this moment. For a while it looked as if she could lose her brother forever, but she was so lucky that she didn't. Throughout everything it was always hard to see her future without Wesley, her only immediate family related by blood. And now, dancing under the stars, she realized how incredibly lucky she was that she did not have to lose him. Kaleigh found herself, standing under the quiet gazebo for a moment, sending up a "thank you" to whomever had led her path in the twists and turns it did to bring her to this moment. Jackson, who had seen her walk away from the tent, decided to give her a few moments alone before joining her.

As soon as Kaleigh had finished her thought, Jackson put his arms around her. She turned around slowly, put her hands on his face and said, "Thank you, for everything," then leaned in for a kiss. When they pulled away he touched her face and said, "Thank you, Mrs. Sanders," and they both smiled. Today had been everything Kaleigh had dreamed of and more.

Before the end of that summer, Wesley and Kaleigh, co-owners of the Garden Center, had made a plan to move forward together. Kaleigh continued teaching full-time, but helped the crew with the flowers, trees and shrubs for a few hours every other Saturday morning, just as she had helped her father. She also worked with a local design team on their logo, and other advertising such as customer appreciation events and donation opportunities. It was important to Kaleigh and Wesley to keep current with the trends and to support their community. They wanted to continue to be THE place to go for everyone's gardening needs while helping to improve the community where they called home.

One night, exactly six months after Jackson and Kaleigh were married, they decided to take Hannah out for ice cream. Afterwards they found themselves walking the pathway at the park, surrounded by twinkle lights as the town prepared for another festival, the two holding hands as they pushed their daughter in a stroller. Kaleigh was again reminded of all the twists and turns that had happened in her life since that first day with Jackson in the gazebo. How for so long she could not see what path she was on at all, or if she would ever find true happiness. While she was experiencing all of the heartache, the loss, it was like her path was clouded over, in a fog that would not allow her to see. During those dark times she could not see where she was or which path she was on. But tonight, in this moment, as she held the hand of her true love and watched their daughter experience the beauty of life, she realized again how lucky she was.

Kaleigh, in this sweet moment, asked Jackson to sit with her on a bench that lined the pathway. Hannah, mesmerized by the lights and her teddy bear, let out a happy squeal. Jackson cherished these special moments with Kaleigh and felt he would never tire of them. He had no idea what was coming, but was sure that anything that came their way, they could handle. And Kaleigh, turning toward her love, taking his hands in hers, shared the news that melted Jackson's heart once again.

"I love our little family more than anything, and you have been such an amazing dad to our Hannah. I can't think of a better father for her and I love taking this journey alongside you." Kaleigh felt the butterflies of excitement inside of her as she spoke.

"I wouldn't want to walk through life with anyone else my Leigh," and he leaned in to kiss her.

When the soft kiss was over, Kaleigh squeezed his hands and asked, "Are you ready for another journey with me?"

Jackson, confused for a moment, replied, "You know I'd go anywhere with you," and smiled,

"Well, for this journey we are going to need another car seat, and a crib . . ." Kaleigh began but Jackson cut her off with a squeal of excitement!

"Are you serious, are you, are we?" He almost couldn't control his emotions.

"Yes, yes!" Kaleigh quickly replied. "I'm pregnant!" And Jackson immediately took her into his arms and hugged her. Then he kissed her, first soft, then long and deep. He was so happy to be having a child with his love. He had imagined someday Kaleigh holding their baby, the two growing their family, and now it was really happening. Hannah let out a squeal of her own and the two turned to her to tell her that she was going to be a big sister!

And at this moment a tear came to Kaleigh's cheek. This time it was a happy one, for it was now that she could truly see how her path had led her here, to this moment, to this beautiful place in her life. All the dark times in the past, the times she felt alone, the times she questioned why things happened, why people left her, walked out on her, those parts of her path were like driving through a storm. In amidst the storms in her life she wondered where she should go, what she should do next, but the storms made it difficult to see. All the lonely nights, every sadness along the path happened for a reason. Even the nightmares were subsiding finally and Kaleigh could see how every defeating moment brought her here. Now that the storms were over, now that everything was clear, she could see what was meant to be, she could see, her path to happiness.

My daughter Madison's drawing

My son Mason's drawing

Author Jennifer Deutsch

I am a Reading Intervention Teacher who lives in upstate New York. I have a hard-working husband who supports all of my endeavors, and two beautiful children who are growing bigger by the day. I work to balance this thing we call life, and it is not always easy. I am constantly looking for easier ways to do things, ways to save time, and stay organized. I work with inner-city students who have so much resting on their shoulders, but who deserve the same chance at becoming great readers and having amazing teachers as any other child in America. I work to show my students how many doors will open for them when they learn how to be great readers. I try to teach my students and my own children that good things come with time, dedication, and hard work.

My family stretches far and wide across the country, and whenever I have the chance to see them, it helps me to remember how precious our family, our life, and our story is.

I consider myself a champion of kindness, and I work everyday to show my kids how to make this world a better place. Life is difficult. I have had my share of curveballs thrown my way. There are things that happen in our lives that try to take away the joy that can be found all around us. Even with all of the trials and roadblocks, I continue to believe in the power of positivity. My own path has been rocky. For so many years I was stuck. I couldn't see where my path might be heading. We may not know for many years why certain things happen and where our path is headed. Our life may seem to be stuck in darkness for so long, but when we come to an overlook, and can see behind us, the purpose of events that happened, the reason certain people entered our lives, that is such a sweet moment. That is a theme in this story, a theme I hope that you can relate to.

My wish is that all of you find your . . . Path to Happiness.